KU-050-820

ACC. No: 02851583

SPECIAL MESSAGE TO READERS

This book is published under the auspices of

THE ULVERSCROFT FOUNDATION

(registered charity No. 264873 UK)

Established in 1972 to provide funds for research, diagnosis and treatment of eye diseases. Examples of contributions made are: —

A Children's Assessment Unit at Moorfield's Hospital, London.

•

Twin operating theatres at the Western Ophthalmic Hospital, London.

•

A Chair of Ophthalmology at the Royal Australian College of Ophthalmologists.

•

The Ulverscroft Children's Eye Unit at the Great Ormond Street Hospital For Sick Children, London.

You can help further the work of the Foundation by making a donation or leaving a legacy. Every contribution, no matter how small, is received with gratitude. Please write for details to:

THE ULVERSCROFT FOUNDATION, The Green, Bradgate Road, Anstey, Leicester LE7 7FU, England. Telephone: (0116) 236 4325

In Australia write to:

THE ULVERSCROFT FOUNDATION, c/o The Royal Australian and New Zealand College of Ophthalmologists, 94-98 Chalmers Street, Surry Hills, N.S.W. 2010, Australia

J. A. O'Brien lives in County Cork, Ireland.

REMAINS FOUND

Two children find a woman's body which is identified first by a friend called Ruby Cox, as Diane Shaft, and later by another friend, Aiden Brooks, as Cecily Staunton. Why did the dead woman have two names? DI Sally Speckle's problems start when Cox vanishes from Loston police station. Then Brooks, claiming he's a clairvoyant, accurately pinpoints the location of where the body was discovered. Does this mean that Brooks is the killer? But as the investigation gets increasingly complicated by troubles far closer to home, followed by another murder, Sally finds she has more suspects than she wants . . .

Books by J. A. O'Brien
Published by The House of Ulverscroft:

PICK UP
OLD BONES

J. A. O'BRIEN

REMAINS FOUND

Complete and Unabridged

ULVERSCROFT
Leicester

First published in Great Britain in 2008 by
Robert Hale Limited
London

First Large Print Edition
published 2009
by arrangement with
Robert Hale Limited
London

British Library CIP Data

O'Brien, J. A. (James A.)
Remains found
1. Women detectives- -Great Britain- -Fiction.
2. Detective and mystery stories. 3. Large type books.
I. Title
823.9′2–dc22

ISBN 978–1–84782–783–8

Published by
F. A. Thorpe (Publishing)
Anstey, Leicestershire

Set by Words & Graphics Ltd.
Anstey, Leicestershire
Printed and bound in Great Britain by
T. J. International Ltd., Padstow, Cornwall

This book is printed on acid-free paper

For my daughter Martina with love.

PROLOGUE

'Wait for me, Ali!'

Alice Sulvane stopped running ahead of her friend and looked back, annoyed. 'What a slowcoach you are, Tina,' she complained. 'You'll have to do better than that to have any chance of qualifyin' for the relay team.'

Tina Croft arrived, panting. 'I ain't sure I want to be in the relay, Ali.'

'You're bein' just lazy, ain't ya. What you need is a better diet.'

'Oh, don't start,' Tina wailed.

'Start what?'

'Tryin' to make me eat rabbit food, of course.'

'Just look at you. You're a mess, ain't ya.'

'That's a bit over the top, Ali Sulvane,' Tina Croft snapped. 'I'm just a coupla pounds heavier than you, that's all.'

'Don't make me laugh,' Ali scoffed.

'Well, we can't all be Miss Perfects, can we?' Tina Croft flung back. 'All shapes and sizes go to make up the world, ya know. And I read somewhere that if you're thin at twelve you'll be tubby at twenty.'

'You talk the most ridiculous tosh,' Ali flung back. 'Now try and keep up, righ'.'

'Can't we walk for a bit?'

'You can,' Ali said, starting off pacily. 'I got a relay race to get ready for.'

'You're not foolin' me, Ali Sulvane. Relay my bum! You're only tryin' to impress Neil Crocker, ain't ya.'

'Don't be daft,' Ali flung back. 'Neil Crocker is a turd.'

'Is that why you sit in class lookin' at him like a sick cow?'

'I do not.'

'Yes, you do.'

'I do not.' Ali Sulvane went sprawling, and accused Tina, 'You tripped me!'

'I did not.'

'Then who did? Ain't no one else 'round. Hopin' I'd break a leg, were you?'

'If you did you could always lean on Neil Crocker!' Tina teased.

'Oh, very clev — '

'Cat got your tongue, then,' Tina said. 'What's the matter? You've gone paler than milk. You've gone and overdone it, ain't ya? You ain't goin' to faint, are ya?'

Ali Sulvane was pointing a shaking finger at a bush she had just passed. 'Lo-lo-look!'

Tina turned and jumped back on seeing a

woman's leg poking out of a bush. Clinging to each other, they looked over the bush to a patch of clear ground behind it.

'Crikey!' Tina Croft exclaimed.

1

DI Sally Speckle picked up the ringing phone. 'I want to report a murder,' said the woman excitedly, the instant she answered.

'May I have your name, please?'

'My name? What do ya want that for?'

'Just for the record.'

'Look, no name, righ'.'

'OK. Where did this murder take place, then?'

'Near the river. That's where Ali and Tina found her.'

'Ali and Tina?'

'They was out runnin'. Gettin' ready for the school relay next week. Ali tripped over this foot pokin' outta the bushes. When they looked behind the bush, there was this woman — dead. Murdered!'

'How do you know she was murdered?' Speckle asked.

'Well, I don't, really. But Ali said she looked all kinda purple.'

'Can you tell me exactly where this was?'

'No. Didn't see her, did I.'

'Is Ali or Tina with you now?'

There was a long silence.

'It would be really helpful if I could talk to either or both,' Sally Speckle said.

'Just a minute.'

There was a muffled conversation in the background. Then a girl said timidly, 'Hello.'

'Ali?' Speckle enquired.

'Yeah.'

'Thanks for coming on the phone to talk to me, Ali. As I was telling your mum,' the girl did not deny the woman was her mother, 'it would be really helpful if you could tell me, or better still show me, where you and Tina found this dead woman?'

'Yeah, I know it would. It's always like that on telly, ain't it.'

'Yes, it is,' Sally Speckle said pleasantly. 'Will you show me?'

The girl went off the line and there was a hushed conversation which Speckle strained to hear but could not. Then the woman came back on the line.

'No, she won't show you.'

'It would save time searching for the body, Mrs . . . ?'

'Sul — ' The woman bit her tongue. Speckle grimaced. She had almost got a name. Still, the chances were that it was Sullivan, something like that. 'Look, I've reported a murder. It's up to you now, ain't it.'

'It's just that in a case of murder, the sooner the police can get the scene secured the better chance there is of finding the killer. The weather forecast is for heavy showers later in the day and that could wash away vital forensic evidence, you see.'

'That's your problem,' the woman said. 'I've done my bit, and me and the kids ain't goin' to get involved no more, righ'.'

The phone went dead.

DI Sally Speckle checked immediately if the number the call was made from had shown up. It had. She jotted it down and phoned it. It rang for a while before it was answered.

'Wha' d'ya want?' a cheeky voice asked. A young boy, Speckle reckoned.

'Can you tell me where that phone is?' the DI enquired of him.

'Why?' The boy was instantly suspicious.

'Wha' is it, Benny?' another boy asked.

'Some bird wantin' to know where the phone is.'

'A bird?' The older boy's interest was instant. 'Give it over, then. Why d'ya wanna know where the phone is?'

In the background a car came up fast.

'OK, then,' a man's voice boomed out, a police officer Speckle guessed. 'Why're you all crowding into that phonebox, then?'

The phone was dropped, crashing against the wall of the phone booth as the boys scattered. She heard the phone being picked up.

'Don't hang up,' she shouted down the line.

But that's exactly what happened. Speckle immediately contacted the telephone company to find out where the phone booth was. A clack of keyboard keys brought an almost instant answer.

'The Clew, Inspector.'

The Clew.

Copper-speak (and evidently also telephone company speak) for the Clewbridge Estate. A sprawling council estate on the south side of Loston, made lawless by a few to the detriment of the many. In recent times the Clew had been renamed 'Asboland' by the officers who patrolled it. The odds were that the caller lived on the estate. Did making the call from the public phone infer that the caller had no phone herself? Or had she taken the precaution of making the call from a public phone to avoid being traced?

Sally Speckle was left with two choices. Find the caller first. Or the body first. The problem was that it was a long stretch of river, much of its length, other than the verges along the riverwalk, wooded and overgrown. A random search would take a lot of manpower (tighter than normal with a tummy bug sweeping through the station) and no small amount of time unless luck favoured the searchers.

DI Sally Speckle looked out the window at the low, scudding clouds driven by a gusting wind. Even if the rain held off, and it didn't look as if it would for very long, the strong gusts of wind would probably sweep away a lot of forensic at the the crime scene. And any trace evidence that would escape the ravages of the wind would probably be degraded by already soggy ground and further rain to come, consequently making it less valuable, less reliable, and open to challenge in court; that was, of course, if the woman's killer was run to ground and brought to trial.

Speckle decided first to try and find the woman who had reported the murder.

She phoned a sergeant she knew in uniform whom she was friendly with and who had, early on in her career, given her a lot of good, common sense advice without any strings attached. 'Jerry. I'm trying to find some people living on the Clewbridge Estate. Does the Clew have community officers?'

'They do, Sally. But they come and go quite a bit. And who'd blame them. Tough stint, the Clew.'

‘Can I have the names and contact numbers of whoever is there now? A murder has been reported by a woman from the public phone on the estate.’

‘A murder in Asboland?’

‘No. Two children found a woman’s body near the river, but we don’t know where. Apparently this woman’s daughter and her friend were out running — ’

‘They’ll have been getting up to speed for the sports day in the grounds of Loston Hospice next Sunday, I expect,’ Sergeant Jerry Cranton said. ‘Mrs Gerrard, the owner and matron of the hospice kindly lets the local youth clubs hold their sports day there. The excitement and ballyhoo of having young people around brightens the residents’ day, Letitia Gerrard says. I’m a volunteer marshal this year.’

It was a benevolent side to Mrs Gerrard that had not been evident during Sally Speckle’s first murder investigation.[1] Then she had been as thorny as a summer rose when the Loston Hospice had figured prominently.

‘And there’s always a special egg and spoon for the oldies.’

Speckle knew of Jerry Cranton’s Trojan work in community affairs, giving much of

---

[1] See: *Pick Up*

his spare time over to organizing one thing or another. In fact, his keen interest in the community he worked in was a throwback to the kind of coppers in *Dixon of Dock Green*; coppers who would have given a youngster a clip behind the ear and set him on the straight and narrow. Nowadays, such an intervention would see the officer severely reprimanded, and the force facing a big compensation payout to parents who would later be visiting their son in jail and mouthing off about the deprivation that had sent him there, with no mention of the lack of parental control which would probably have prevented it.

'Look, why don't I arrange for the lads to meet up with you in the Clew,' Cranton offered. 'Say at the public phone?'

'Great. Thanks, Jerry. How is Margaret?'

He chuckled. 'Like all wives, demanding. You haven't been round to the house for an age.'

'I'll drop by soon.'

'Is that a promise?'

'That's a promise. One of the girl's name was Ali, probably short for Alice. The other girl's name was Tina. And the surname begins Sul — S U L. Sullivan? Possibly something like.'

'That'll probably point us in the right direction. And if it doesn't, there's always the sports day list of names and events which I've got at home. If they've been training for the relay, they'll be on that, I shouldn't wonder. And the chances are that the girls are probably members of the Clewbridge Youth Club, Sally.'

Speckle laughed. 'Maybe you should be the detective, Jerry.'

'I'd phone Margaret for the list right off, but she's away in Manchester visiting with her sister Beth. If we draw a blank, I'll give someone the key and they can go round to the house and get the list.'

'Thanks, Jerry. Tell Margaret I said hello.'

'I will. She'll appreciate you asking. And you must come round to see her latest artwork.'

'Artwork?'

'Yeah. She's taken to sticking cuttings from old and recent newspapers on a sheet of plywood with this nose-blocking glue to show how, in reality, life and people change little. When you see the cuttings laid out you'd be surprised how right she is. Has our neighbours bothered out of their wits collecting old newspapers from everyone's loft and garage.'

'Interesting.'

'Bloody daft, you mean.'

'Look on the bright side, Jerry. It'll

probably sell for a fortune.'

'The sooner the better. It's cluttering up the spare room, where I keep my photo collections.'

'By now you'd need a warehouse for that I'd imagine.' Jerry Cranton was known in the Loston nick as Sergeant Snap-it, due to his obsession with photography. 'Didn't you have a darkroom built out back?'

'Yes.'

'So why don't you keep your photo collection in there?'

'And risk vandalism? Never! Margaret was chuffed to hear that you'd been made a DI, Sally. She said that you were the only copper whose brain had been put in the right place and with the correct connections.'

Speckle laughed. 'A shrewd woman, your Margaret.'

Sally Speckle had visited with the Crantons a couple of times, and had thought Margaret Cranton pleasant and very good company. And it was obvious that her world revolved around her husband, and his around hers.

'Too much so,' had been Andy Lukeson's opinion, expressed at a retirement bash. 'I don't know how Jerry sticks being suffocated the way he is.'

'Jerry doesn't seem to mind,' had been her observation.

'All I can say is that I hope he doesn't ever

do anything to break those rose-tinted glasses she sees him through.'

As if reading her thoughts, Cranton asked, 'How's Andy Lukeson?'

'He's fine. At the moment away on a course entitled: 'What It Means To Be a Criminal Investigator'. Given by a guest lecturer from the NYPD.'

'Who picks up the bill for that?'

'I'm not sure.'

Jerry Cranton chuckled. 'If Frank Doyle throws himself from his ivory tower, you'll know Loston had to fork up. A man to watch every penny, our Chief Super. Well, best let you brainy ones get on with it, then. You head over to Asboland then, Sally.'

Putting down the phone, Speckle thought that it was a shame that Jerry Cranton had not had kids, because he would have made a marvellous father.

She checked if anyone had been reported missing and drew a blank. She went to the door of her office and called out to DC Helen Rochester who was writing up a report on a series of car thefts in the upper-class range of vehicles, the latest of which was a Jaguar.

Helen Rochester set the report aside to answer her DI's summons.

'Looks like we have a murder on our hands, Helen,' Speckle said. 'Two young girls found a woman's body at some point along the river while out running.'

'At some point along the river? Can't they be more specific?'

'Oh, it's the classic case of not wanting to get involved. The mum of one of the girls phoned in. But that was that as far as she was concerned.'

'Bloody typical,' Rochester groaned. 'How would she like it if it was her daughter or sister they had found.'

'The woman comes from a police-hostile environment, Helen. The Clewbridge Estate.'

'Clewbridge! Helping a copper on the Clew is like bringing Satan home to tea in a nunnery. Why do they build places like that, pile people in, and then just let the place rot? A youngster growing up in the Clew hasn't got a chance of a decent life.'

'Jerry Cranton is making arrangments for us to meet with a community officer.'

'Anyone reported missing?'

'No.'

'Shall I organize a search of the river bank?'

'We're pretty short on manpower right now. That tummy bug doing the rounds is creating havoc. And Andy Lukeson is off on a stupid course. Why do the powers that be have to send people off on courses when we're so short of manpower,' the DI complained. 'Makes no bloody sense.'

'I suppose if the brass had to wait until we had sufficient manpower, even at the best of times, no one ever would be on a course,' Rochester reasoned. Raindrops spattered the window. 'Not weather to leave a body lying around in for long, is it.'

'It's Hobson's choice, isn't it,' Speckle said dourly. 'Even if we had a search party of a hundred they could search for a long time before finding the body. Near town, the council keeps the river banks in reasonable shape, but further out it's a bit of a mess. Enough nooks and crannies to hide a small army in, let alone one body.'

'Well, at least it's late autumn. Be a lot worse if it was leafy.'

'There'll be a lot of decaying vegetation to wade through.'

'The body can't be too much out of the way, if kids found it.'

'Kids can wander off anywhere, Helen.'

'Not now, not in the world we live in. Kids are always being warned to avoid out-of-the-way places.'

'These are Clewbridge youngsters, Helen. They're probably used to looking after themselves.'

'That's a bit unfair, isn't it?' Rochester

protested. 'Some on the Clewbridge hardly deserve to be called human. But there are good people there too; people who just couldn't afford anything else. It's not fair to tar everyone with the same brush.'

DI Sally Speckle stood justly admonished. And she wondered how much the generalization she had just made showed her degree of being sucked into the police establishment when she had made herself a promise that she would not be.

'Sorry if I spoke out of turn,' DC Helen Rochester said.

'No. You're right. Above all else, a police officer should not tar everyone with the same brush. We'd best head for Clewbridge.' Leaving her office, Speckle asked, 'Any breakthrough yet on those auto thefts?'

Rochester's shoulders slumped. 'It's as if aliens have nicked the cars off the face of the earth. The latest, a Jaguar. The owner parked the car, went into the house to collect something, came back out almost immediately and the Jag had vanished.'

'Didn't he hear it being nicked?'

'Says he didn't hear a thing.'

'Was the car parked a good distance from the house?'

'No. At the front door.'

'A big house, is it?'

‘Knock it down and you have Old Trafford; big.’

‘And where was he in the house when it was stolen. Front or rear?’

‘Didn’t ask?’ Rochester admitted. ‘But now I see the significance of that question. If he was to the front of the house he’d have had to have heard. Give me a sec.’ Rochester diverted to her desk to get Alex Crick’s phone number from file and called him. A moment later, back with Speckle, after attaching a hurried note to the car theft file, she said, ‘Says he was in a room just inside the door.’

‘Curious.’ Speckle walked on. ‘Oh, you’ll be Acting DS until Andy Lukeson gets back, Helen.’

‘Me?’

‘Yes. Is that a problem?’

‘No.’

But Helen Rochester feared that it would very likely be one hell of a problem.

* * *

As they drove into the Clewbridge Estate the sun made a brief appearance, but Sally Speckle thought that had it been high summer instead of late autumn it would have made no difference to the pall of depression that was the lot of those unfortuante enough to have to live on the Clew. A burned-out car sat dead centre of a green area that had long ago been abandoned as a lost cause. Empty beer cans were strewn about and litter bins, like the car on the green, had been set on fire by vandals. Graffiti, most of it lewd or anti-establishment, occupied every spare inch of wall.

'Bloody awful, isn't it?' Helen Rochester said gloomily.

'Not pretty,' Speckle agreed.

'Should bulldoze the lot.'

'Wouldn't do much good, unless the underlying reason for places like the Clew-bridge are dealt with,' Speckle opined.

'They know we're coppers,' Rochester said, driving past a group of children who were clearly the vandals of the future in the making. 'They can smell a copper round here.'

A stone bounced off the roof of the Punto and in the rearview mirror Speckle saw the children scatter.

'Stop the car and I'll — '

'No point in starting something, when we're here looking for help to find that woman's body,' Speckle said.

A squad car rounding a corner flashed its headlights and drew alongside the Punto. 'DI Speckle?' the driver enquired.

'Yes, I'm Speckle.'

'PC Bracken, ma'am. Jerry Cranton told us to look out for a Punto that should have been scrapped long ago.'

Sally Speckle laughed. 'Jerry Cranton is a cheeky sod.'

'The Sulvanes have a daughter called Ali, so I reckon they're who you're looking for. Block four. Flat 67. Follow me, ma'am.'

The squad car's turn would have done any joyrider proud and it raced ahead, too fast in Speckle's opinion. When they stopped, she thought it only proper to bring Bracken's attention to his driving.

'You have to move lively here, ma'am,' he said, unapologetic. 'If you don't, you'll get a brick through your windscreen.'

Sally Speckle thought of the stoning incident a couple of minutes before, understood, and accepted PC Bracken's point of view.

'Want me to lead the way, ma'am?' Bracken asked.

'No, I think it would be best if we went alone. Uniforms might have an adverse effect.'

'A copper's a copper to this lot,' Bracken said. 'Civvies or uniform.'

The DI led the way into block four and was even more depressed. It stank of stale urine and beer. 'The stairs,' she said, on seeing that the lift had been used as a toilet. On the third step of the stairs, Rochester recoiled as glass crunched underfoot and she saw a used syringe, it's needle stained with dried blood. A used condom hung by a piece of string from a light fitting with a handwritten note attached that read: I screwed Sarah Gibbons with this johnnie. Pity I put a hole in it first. Hah! Hah!

Flat 67 had a door that bore the marks of something blunt having been used on it. There was no knocker and no bell. Sally Speckle used her fist to hammer on the door. Knocking would have been useless to overcome the loud music inside the flat. On the fourth combined hammering of fists by Speckle and Rochester the music was toned down and seconds later the door of the flat was yanked open.

'Mum. Filth!' the teenage boy shouted back into the flat. He turned and walked away, colliding with a harrassed-looking woman, way older than the years her birth certificate would state, Speckle reckoned, coming from another room. 'Don't take any shit from 'em, mum,' the boy said. He turned into a room further along and instantly the wall-shattering music was back, even more deafening that before. The woman looked hopelessly to the room, thought about doing something, and then clearly decided that she would be wasting her time.

'Mrs Sulvane?' Speckle enquired above the racket.

'It's about that body my Ali found, innit?'

* * *

Ali Sulvane and Tina Croft led the way, with DI Sally Speckle and DC Helen Rochester trying to keep pace with their more agile leaders. Mrs Sulvane was bringing up the rear a good distance behind. The path wound away into a narrower and darker track.

'Better wait for your mum to catch up, Ali,' Speckle said. 'And then we'll go a bit slower, eh.'

Breathless, Mrs Sulvane caught them up.

'It's the ciggies,' she said. 'Must give 'em up. And I told you, young lady, to stick to the main path, didn't I,' she rebuked Ali. She looked around her at the creepy off-shoot. 'What if that woman's murderer was still 'round here. You both could have been done in.'

'Your mum is right, Ali,' Speckle said. 'Best to stay out of places like this. OK to go on, Mrs Sulvane?'

'Yeah. Best get it over with.'

'Slowly,' Speckle said, when the girls picked up the pace again.

Reaching the top of a mossy rise, the ground dipped, leading down into thick undergrowth. Ali declared, pointing, 'There. Behind that bush.'

Speckle and Rochester went forward, but found no body.

'She was here,' Ali said. 'I swear she was.'

'You ain't been havin' one of them flights of fancy you sometimes have?' Mrs Sulvane questioned her daughter.

'No, I ain't mum. I tell ya she was — '

'I don't know, Ali,' Tina Croft doubted.

'Where do you think she was, Tina?' Speckle encouraged.

'I think there was 'nother path, kinda goin' off that way.' She pointed to her right.

'Well, why don't we see.'

'Follow me,' Tina said cockily, now that she was the centre of attention.

'You don't know what you're talkin' about,' Ali Sulvane charged.

'Yes, I do so,' Tina flung back annoyedly.

'We'll see,' Ali said sullenly.

'Yeah, we'll see,' Tina said, throwing back her head of long black hair. A couple of minutes on, she said confidently, and proved to be as good as her word, 'See.' She pointed to a woman's ankle, adorned with an expensive flame-red shoe and a silver ankle chain, poking out of a bush. 'Told you, didn't I, Ali Sulvane.'

2

DS Andy Lukeson was trying to remain attentive, but after a decent lunch the lecturer's New York drawl and his repetitive re-stating of what was already routine practice (but which he was trying to purvey as new and enlightened thinking), made it almost impossible to resist his drowsiness.

'Andy!'

Lukeson jerked awake from a doze, and for a second wondered how he was seeing the lecturer sideways, until he realized that his head was on a colleague's shoulder.

'People will talk,' said Jack Stack, a DI in Brigham CID, Loston's neighbour. 'Boring old fart, isn't he,' he opined of the representative from NYPD. 'Finishes almost every sentence with,' Stack did a perfect mimic of the New Yorker, 'we in the NYPD.'

Stack chuckled.

'Like his Girl Friday, though.'

Andy Lukeson had to agreee. When it came to design and desirability, Shannon Doherty had been at the front of the queue.

'Heard Harry Burke tried it on with her last night,' Stack said. 'Almost caught pneumonia from the frost.'

' . . . We in the NYPD,' the lecturer intoned, yet again.

'See what I mean,' Stack complained. 'I don't think I can take much more of this shite. All of this is just a con for senior officers to go off on junkets. My super is currently in Barbados doing there what this ponce from New York is doing here!'

Jack Stack chuckled throatily.

'But on the other hand it has its compensations, Andy,' he said, when Shannon Doherty, complete with the obligatory red hair and green eyes of her Irish ancestry, dropped a sheaf of notes and bent to pick them up. Her boss glanced furiously at her, because at that moment he knew that he had lost an audience who were less than enthusiastic to begin with. Soon after, he wound up the lecture with the announcement, 'After the coffee break, I'll show you guys how we work the crime scene in — '

'The NYPD,' Stack drawled.

* * *

A PC taped off the crime scene with the familiar blue and white tape while a colleague erected a tent over the woman's body, taking in the bush from which her leg poked. Both then joined a third colleague to keep the increasing number of onlookers well away.

'Amazing, isn't it,' Helen Rochester said. 'No matter how out of the way a body is found, within minutes there's a crowd.'

Arc lamps lit the scene, giving the gloomy path and the surrounding area a ghostly feel. DI Sally Speckle thought: At least the remains aren't skeletal.[1] 'Send them packing, before they plod on every bit of forensic there is,' she told the officers protecting the crime scene.

'All right, then,' said the senior of the three. 'There's nothing here to see. So be on your way.'

A freelance photo journalist, formerly of the Loston Echo, had shrewdly cornered Ali Sulvane and her mother, a meeting which Speckle quickly intervened in. 'I don't think it's wise to make any comment yet, Mrs Sulvane,' she advised, 'that might impede the police investigation. An officer will see you safely home. We'll take a statement later Ali, if that's okay with you and your mum?'

'A statement!' Ali squealed. 'Just like on The Bill?'

Sally Speckle smiled. 'Something like that, yes.'

---

[1] See: *Old Bones*.

Ali Sulvane shot a superior look at Tina Croft.

'And, of course, we'll also need a statement from you, Tina,' Speckle added.

In turn, Tina Croft returned Ali Sulvane's look of superiority, adding a good fifty per cent.

The SOCOs were already in situ and Speckle was awaiting the arrival of Alec Balson, the police surgeon. He had been summoned half an hour ago, but it being surgery hours delay was inevitable. There had often been heated debate about the feasibilty of having a GP (whose first committments were to the living, instead of a pathologist who dealt with the dead and could arrive on scene more quickly) doubling as a police surgeon. And there was an argument to be made for such because, though the observations of a good police surgeon (and Alec Balson was one of the best) at the scene of the crime were invaluable in the early stages of an investigation, it fell to the forensic pathologist to provide the finer detail that often made the difference between failure and success.

'Hope it won't rain before Balson gets here,' the SOCO team leader complained.

'Fingers crossed,' Speckle said.

The DI checked again to find out if a woman had been reported missing, but no one had been. The dead woman had no ID on her, and a positive identification would save precious time lost in having to find out who she was, before the investigation proper could begin. And Speckle was only too aware of how important a quick and smooth start to any investigation was.

Alec Balson came into view along the path, escorted by a PC, trying in vain to match the sure-footedness and pace of the younger constable.

'That lad should be an Olympic sprinter,' the police surgeon groused to Speckle. 'He'd have taken gold without a doubt.' He looked into the tent covering the woman's body. 'Nasty.' He went inside to begin his examination, joined by Speckle.

'First impressions, Alec.'

On her third murder investigation, Alec Balson had become a friend.

'By her facial expression, she could have died from pure terror. But,' he opened her mouth to examine it and then her nostrils, both having a degree of what looked like grey toffee clinging to them, 'she could have choked to death.'

'Choked?' Speckle asked doubtfully. 'Natural causes, then?'

'Oh, no. She was murdered all right. See this stuff here,' he indicated her mouth and nose with his finger. 'Glue. The killer blocked her air passages with glue, Sally. Must have been a hard death, if short in coming. Hence the look of terror on the poor woman's face. Struggling for breath and knowing that you're not going to get it would do that.'

He examined a bruise on her temple.

'Stunned first, I'd say. To allow the killer to stuff her full of glue, I shouldn't wonder.'

'Time of death?'

'Difficult. But she's been dead for a couple of days. Has she been reported missing?'

'No.'

'A beautiful woman like her, you'd think someone would miss her?'

'Might be living alone.'

'She's married.' He pointed to the indentation of a ring on her wedding finger. 'Or was up to very recently. The indentation of the ring, still strong, suggests that.'

'Maybe she still was,' Speckle observed. 'She might have taken her ring off for a night out? Or to meet a lover?'

Balson chuckled. 'It's only the devious mind of a woman would think that. Abroad recently, too.'

'It could be a sunbed tan.'

'Natural,' Balson said.

Sally Speckle called Balson's attention to

circular shading on her ankles and wrists. 'Bound?'

'Hand and foot. Seems to me that there was a lot of cruelty or vindictiveness in her killing,' Balson observed. 'You're looking for a sadistic bastard, Sally. A killer who liked to watch his victim die, I reckon.'

'Not good news,' Speckle said. 'If he likes watching, he could kill again. Any sign of sexual activity?'

'Strangely doesn't seem to be. At least nothing that is that obvious. Time has passed, of course. I'll take some swabs.' Balson looked steadily at Sally Speckle. 'You could be up against it this time, Sally. Andy Lukeson's off on a junket, I hear.'

'Brighton.'

'Nice for some, eh.'

Could it be Alec Balson's opinion that the difficulty of the task facing her had been made all the more onerous because of Lukeson's absence? Speckle wondered.

'I want every inch of this place finger-tipped, Helen,' Speckle said. 'And beyond to at least that tree for starters.' She pointed to a far oak.

'Comment, Inspector?'

Sally Speckle swung round on a smallish man with a head that bobbed on his shoulders like a puppet's, the former photograher with the *Loston Echo*, now a freelance photo journalist as he liked to descibe himself. He had taken advantage of the PCs while they pushed back the crowd to duck under the tape.

'You're not supposed to be here, Loss,' Speckle snapped. 'And you've been around enough crime scenes to know that.'

One of the PCs came hurrying over. 'Sorry, ma'am. Just turned me back for the blink of an eye.' He grabbed Loss.

'How did he get here so fast?' Rochester wondered.

'Wait,' Speckle ordered the PC. 'Hand over your shoes for forensic testing, Loss.'

'Don't be daft,' Loss protested.

'Come on, then,' the PC growled. 'Hand 'em over.'

'This is police harassment,' Loss protested, but handed over his runners. Because he knew that finding an excuse for intruding on a crime scene, with twenty-five years as a crime reporter behind him, would be hard to explain or excuse up before a magistrate.

'What've you got in here?' the PC complained, on receiving the shoes. 'Raw sewage.'

'You haven't heard the last of this,' Loss, warned Speckle. 'And what if I pick up something dodgy from standing round in my stockinged feet, eh?'

'There's nothing around here that could possibly act as a contaminant where you're concerned, Loss,' Speckle flung back. 'You wouldn't have a spare pair of wellies you could loan Mr Loss, have you?' Speckle enquired of the SOCO team leader.

'Probably a pair in the van.'

'Go get them, Constable,' the DI ordered the PC.

'The press has rights, you know,' Loss complained.

'Oh, don't go on,' Speckle barked. 'You illegally entered a crime scene. And the person whose rights need to be protected round here is the woman who has been brutally murdered.'

Loss went to continue his protest.

'Arrest him,' Speckle told the second PC.

'You can't do that,' Loss complained, knowing very well that she could and probably would, too. 'OK,' he held up his hands in a truce. 'But could I have those wellies fast before something bloody queer kills me?'

'I doubt if there's anything malignant enough to kill you, Loss,' Speckle said.

'Oh, very funny, Inspector. That's what a college education will do for you?'

Sally Speckle bristled at Loss's mention of

a college education. During the Pick Up case, her first murder investigation, Loss had photographed her in a pensive mood and had added the caption:

A PENNY FOR YOUR THOUGHTS,
INSPECTOR. THAT IS IF YOU HAVE ANY?

He then went on to write a piece about the relevance of a university education in solving a murder, cashing in on an ongoing debate about the value of the police graduate entrants scheme, and those 'graddies' (the disparaging term for graduates) taking promotions from good, honest coppers.

DI Sally Speckle took her mobile phone from her coat pocket. She had been tossing up ever since she had discovered the woman's body if she'd phone Andy Lukeson. Now she had decided to do so, because this, her third murder investigation, was the first case that she had not had his advice and indeed comradeship.

'Andy. Hi, Sally.'

* * *

NYPD looked down from the podium, annoyed by the ringing tone (the *1812 Overture*) of Andy Lukeson's phone. NYPD paused, letting the silence get the full benefit of the Overture before Lukeson answered. Then his gaze went to Chief Superintdent Arthur Glass of Brigham CID, the ranking officer and the course organizer, whose face clouded over like a stormy sky. He turned in his seat and glared back. Lukeson waved his hands in an 'aren't I an idiot' gesture which, judging by Glass's hostile glare, he was in full agreement with. CS Glass's eyes flicked towards the sign that read: PLEASE SWITCH OFF ALL MOBILE PHONES. Lukeson left the room with the stealth of an assassin after the deed has been done. 'As I was saying. We in the NYPD . . . ' Lukeson closed the door behind him gently.

'Andy?'

'Yeah.'

'Sorry. Have I dropped you in it?'

'Up to my armpits. I'll probably be shot at dawn. And I wouldn't half mind. It would be blessed relief from having to listen to that boring fart from NYPD.'

'Sorry, again.'

'Don't be. I was just about to top myself when you phoned.'

'That bad?'

'Add fifty per cent to your worst thoughts,' he said.

'Then say thanks, Sally,' Speckle chirped.

‘Thanks, Sally. Now, what’s happened? Don’t tell me, ‘Sermon’ Doyle has chucked himself out the window because of last month’s overtime figures.’

‘No. Not quite.’

‘And I thought you were ringing with good news.’

‘We’ve had a murder, Andy. A real nasty one, too. A woman. And the killer was a sadistic bastard who blocked her air passages with glue.’

‘I’m on my way back.’

‘No. No need.’

‘If you say so,’ Lukeson said cooly, disappointed that Sally Speckle had not called to request his return; a request that would have been readily granted if made. He had no doubt that NYPD would be glad to see the back of him, as would Glass, as would he they.

‘You’ll be back by the end of the week anyway,’ Speckle said, making her tone upbeat, sensing Lukeson’s disappointment. She knew she had cocked up and tried to cover, but she suspected it had not worked. She had phoned more or less to talk about the murder, to share her thoughts and get his feedback, not to seek Lukeson’s return, much as she’d like his input into the investigation.

‘ID, have you?’ he asked, trying for a casual

tone of voice, but not quite succeeding.

'Not yet. No ID on her.'

'No one missing her?'

'No.'

'How long dead?'

'Alec Balson's initial estimate is a couple of days.'

'Should have been missed by someone by now. Unless she's homeless?'

'Not wearing the expensive gear she's wearing.'

'Glue, you said?'

'Yes. Common as muck, too. Thousands of tubes sold every week, I shouldn't wonder.'

'Stands out from your normal stab or bash affair. Maybe she hasn't been reported because the person who could report her missing is her killer, Sally. You know how it is. Relatives report people lost if they don't come home for tea.'

The conversation came to a natural end, because there was nothing to discuss beyond that point with the inquiry just getting off the ground. That being the case, Sally Speckle began to think about why she had phoned Andy Lukeson? And she dared not think that the real reason for her call might not be strictly in the interests of police work.

'Give my regards to old Broadway, Andy,' she said brightly. 'Bye.'

The call had left Sally Speckle with mixed feelings. She was glad she had phoned Andy Lukeson. But on the other hand, she regretted the awkward bit, because Lukeson had assumed that she was going to call him back. Now she hoped that she had not damaged their working relationship and, more importantly their friendship, which she valued greatly.

'Are you and Andy Lukeson an item?' a colleague had recently asked. 'Because if you are,' she had gone on before Speckle could deny it, 'it'll cause all sorts of grief in both your work life and home life. Bad enough having to argue at work, without having to continue at home because of work.' The colleague who had given the advice had been well placed to do so, having had two in-house relationships that had ended acrimoniously. 'You know,' she had said sagely, 'the last person to understand a copper's lot is a copper.'

Sally Speckle had a feeling that there had been talk.

'It's a lot better if one or both are married or at least in a permanent relationship. It saves on awkward situations,' her colleague had advised.

'Then maybe I should go off and take a husband,' Speckle had replied flippantly, which really did no good at all. Because it would only give grist to the rumour mill.

'Let's get back to the station, Helen,' she said. 'Nothing much more we can do here but stand around. Give me all you've got as soon as possible,' she requested of the SOCO team leader.

'What about my runners?' Ed Loss asked, now wearing a pair of official police wellies. 'When can I have them back.'

DI Sally Speckle ignored his question.

* * *

When Speckle arrived back at the station, the desk sergeant beckoned to her. 'Woman over there,' he let his eyes go beyoned Speckle to a woman, close in age to the murdered woman, 'says she thinks she knows who the murdered woman is, ma'am.'

Sally Speckle turned round and smiled at the woman whom, she noted with interest, was every inch as well turned out as the dead woman had been. No cheap rags for these women, she noted.

'DI Sally Speckle. I believe you have some information that may be of help.'

'I heard that there was a woman's body found near the river. Is that right?'

'Heard?'

'A friend who was out for a walk along the river path — ' Sally Speckle took this with a pinch of salt. 'Is it true?'

'Yes.'

'Murdered, was she?'

'What's this information?' Speckle hedged.

'Are you the officer in charge of the murder investigation?' the woman asked, nervously shuffling her feet.

'Murder investigation?'

'It must be. A woman found dead near the river.'

'Many people die in strange places of natural causes, Ms? Mrs?'

'Cox. Ruby Cox. Must be, murder, I mean. I told her. I said, Diane watch your step. Now she's dead.'

'Diane?' Speckle probed.

'Diane Shaft, at least I think so. Blonde. The genuine article, not the bottle variety. Blue eyes. Wearing a red outfit, a very expensive red outfit. Shoes to match. Silver ankle chain on her right leg.'

'That pretty much describes the dead woman, yes,' Speckle confirmed. 'Is *Mrs* Shaft a friend of yours?' the DI asked, recalling that the dead woman had up to recently been wearing a wedding ring.

'I suppose you might say that.'

She had not questioned that the murdered

woman was married. And Speckle wondered why Cox, who was a friend of the dead woman *you might say*, had reported her missing rather than her husband, when she had been dead a couple of days?

'Mrs Shaft's husband — ?'

'Gone.'

'Gone? You mean left her?'

'No.' Ruby Cox pointed to the ceiling.

'Dead?'

'Yes.'

'Recently?'

'A month. Six weeks, maybe. Out walking on the cliffs some place in Devon and fell off. Used to go off walking all over the place on his own, did Roger.'

'Tragic.'

'Not for Diane. She'd been trying to unload him for years.'

'I see.' Speckle paused for just the right time, before asking in as casual a manner as she could, 'Was Diane on this cliff walk with her husband?'

'God, no. She wouldn't cross the road with him. Look, I've got to go. Someone waiting for me.'

'Family?'

'No kids. Just Roger.'

'Relatives, then?'

'Diane never said.'

'You said that you told Diane to watch her step. Why was that? Was she in some kind of danger?'

'The bloke she had shacked up with. Odd in the head, if you ask me. Now, I've really got to go.'

'We'll need someone to formally identify the body.'

'Oh, I don't think I'd fancy doing that. Look, maybe it isn't Diane at all,' she said desperately. 'You'll have to get someone else. Sorry.'

Not getting anywhere with her softly softly approach, DI Sally Speckle decided to become more official in tone and manner. 'This is a murder inquiry. So you're duty bound to tell us everything you know about Diane Shaft. Otherwise you could lay yourself open to a charge of witholding information. Even impeding a murder inquiry,' the DI ended ominously.

'I shouldn't have come here.'

Sally Speckle softened her tone. 'But now that you have, you can really be of help. Help we will much appreciate. You'd want Diane's killer caught, wouldn't you?'

'Of course I would.'

'Then — '

'Just a quick peek, maybe. What's that?' Cox asked, startled by the fire alarm sounding. 'What's happening?' she quickly added as doors burst open and staff flooded through into the reception area.

'Just a fire drill, I expect. Nothing to worry about.'

'Everyone out,' shouted Sergeant Harry Bowe from uniform, one of the station fire marshals. 'Come on, then. Let's be having you,' he shouted at Speckle. 'Move it.'

A fire drill was one of the few occasions when a junior officer was empowered to order a senior colleague, and Harry Bowe relished the opportunity.

'Keep your shirt on, Sergeant,' Speckle said. She turned back to Cox. 'This is just a temporary — ' But Ruby Cox was gone. Speckle hurried outside, but there was no sign of Cox. She recalled a red car that had been parked at the corner of the street when she had come in, the driver, a man, with his seat belt still on. Which indicated that he was not expecting to be waiting for very long. Speckle reckoned that the car had been waiting for Cox. She glanced up at the CCTV cameras above the station entrance. One was beamed directly on the entrance. There were two others set at angles to cover the street either side of the approach to the station, and she wondered if the camera covering the lower half of the street, where the car had been parked (she had a vague recollection of a Renault Megane), had recorded it. If it had, enhanced, at least the man's profile might be visible. But not the registration number, because the side of the car would have been facing the camera.

Ten minutes later the all clear sounded. Sally Speckle was still bemoaning the unfortunate timing of the fire alert.

'Some twat dropped the butt of his ciggie into the waste bin in the public loo,' Bowe told her. 'Bin smouldered.'

Going upstairs, she told Acting DS Helen Rochester. 'Move heaven and hell to find Cox. That new CCTV camera above the desk sergeant's desk should give us a good picture of her. And check the CCTV tape from outside the station, the camera facing down the street, for a car parked at the corner, red in colour and probably a Renault Megane. Hopefully the angle of the camera was not too acute and we'll get some good footage to enhance.

'I was out the door almost immediately after Cox and she had vanished, but the car was gone. So the parked car must be the answer. If there's no useful CCTV footage, start checking on Coxes and red Meganes in Loston and the surrounding area.'

'There'll be a lot of Coxes and even more

Meganes,' Rochester said.

Turning into her office, the DI said, 'That's what makes police work such a joy, Helen.' Flopping into the chair behind her desk, Sally Speckle took some consolation in the fact that at least the inquiry had gotten off the ground.

She phoned DC Charlie Johnson and told him to report for duty.

'It's my day off, boss,' he complained in a whisper.

'Charlie.' The sound of a shower from the recently installed en suite which Charlie Johnson had bored everyone with, came down the line as the shower door was opened. 'Do be a darling and wash my back,' the woman cooed.

'Sorry, Charlie,' Speckle said. 'But murder comes first. An hour from now, shall we say?' She hung up before Johnson could protest further. 'Enter,' she called out to whoever had knocked on the frosted glass door of her office, a man by shape, unless a female wrestler had joined the staff. The door opened to reveal DS Ben George, not a visitor she would welcome and, likewise, George would not want to see her either.

When she had been in Administration, before she had been made a DI, George and she had had a fiery altercation about some forms he should have filed, which he had not filed, but swore he had. George was also critical of graduate entrants to the police leap-frogging to promotion (as he saw it, and he was not alone in that view) to make senior officers look good in the eyes of their superiors, who in turn wanted to look good in the eyes of the Whitehall mandarins.

'One big bloody happy family of wankers, the lot!' Ben George had been heard to say when, for the third time, he had been passed over for promotion, a promotion that on his record and manner, if both did not radically improve, would continue to pass him by. As a result of all of this, Speckle and George avoided each other as much as was possile.

'A report about a missing woman,' he said surlily. 'Probably the one who got herself topped.'

'I believe we've already identified her, Sergeant. But thanks for letting me know, anyway.'

'Blonde hair. Blue eyes. Expensive clobber. Silver ankle chain.'

Speckle was stunned. What were the odds on two missing women with blonde hair, blue eyes, expensive clothes and a silver ankle chain — astronomical.

'Someone taking the piss, you reckon, ma'am?' Ben George said smugly, sensing

Speckle's surprise.

'Who reported the woman missing?'

'The bloke says he's her,' his mouth curled cynically, '*friend*.'

'Address and phone number?'

'No.'

'Didn't you ask, sergeant?' she asked tersely.

George had baited her, and he enjoyed his little triumph. 'He's right here in reception. Says his name is Aiden Brooks.'

'I'll be right down.'

'Ma'am,' George intoned sarcastically.

DS Ben George was one of the old school coppers, who had little if any time for graduate entrants and had been heard to refer to them as 'poshies'.

'It's understandable that Ben George should be sour,' Lukeson had recently said in his defence. 'He's been jumped twice for promotion by 'poshies'.'

'Don't you start that shit, Andy,' she had flung back. 'George wasn't promoted because of his sick record and two charges of dereliction of duty. And his Atilla the Hun attitude.'

'I know,' Lukeson had conceded. 'But try telling Ben George that. As far as he's concerned he's still a sergeant because a couple of your lot were favoured by the brass and got the promotion he deserved.'

'Is that your opinion, too?' she had challenged Lukeson.

'No. But I understand how George and others might think so.'

The disagreement over Ben George had been the only one between herself and Andy Lukeson, the only ruffle in what had been, in the general opinion of their CID colleagues, an excellent partnership.

* * *

'Mr Brooks?'

The man reading a travel book (not greatly concerned about a missing friend, it would appear) looked up. 'Cambodia,' he said, holding up the book. 'A very interesting and beautiful country.'

'Not really my taste,' Speckle said conversationally. 'I more or less stick to Europe.'

'No sense of adventure, then?' he asked pleasantly.

'Right old stick-in-the-mud, that's me.'

'And you are?'

'DI Sally Speckle.'

'Pleased to meet you.'

Brooks held out his hand which Sally Speckle shook, but she did not like the sweaty feel of it and took her hand back as quickly as was decent when Brooks seemed to want to hold on to it. An inexplicable, unpleasant little shiver ran through her.

'You've reported your *friend* missing?'

'Yes, Inspector.'

'And her name is?'

'Staunton. Cecily Staunton.'

'Staunton?'

'You seem surprised, Inspector?'

'Will you please describe Ms Staunton for me?' Speckle asked, with a sinking feeling.

'Blonde. Blue eyes. About five foot eight. Well dressed. Oh, and she'll have been wearing a silver ankle chain. Never went anywhere without an ankle chain.'

'How long has Ms Staunton been missing, Mr Brooks?'

'Cecily is a widow. Husband fell off a cliff, silly bugger. Three days, I mean since I last saw her, and please call me Aiden.' He held Sally Speckle's gaze, and she felt uncomfortable under his scrutiny, feeling herself naked.

'Why didn't you report Mrs Staunton missing before now?'

'I was . . . *away*.'

'Away where, Mr Brooks?'

'I'd rather not say, Inspector. It was a very private and personal matter.' He frowned, the deep lines in his forehead suddenly making him look older by adding maturity to his otherwise round, soft face. 'I have this feeling, Inspector — '

'What feeling would that be, Mr Brooks?'

'Well, a feeling of something being wrong — terribly wrong, in fact.'

'Regarding Mrs Staunton?'

'Yes. I'm a clairvoyant. Not professional in a show business sense, you understand,' he added hastily, clearly not thinking much of theatrical clairvoyants. 'But since childhood I get a sense of foreboding that always heralds in bad news, I'm afraid. Like the foreboding I'm feeling now.'

His dark eyes bore into Speckle.

'You see, Inspector. I think that Cecily has passed over. There's a chill about me. There always has been when someone close to me dies.'

Ruby Cox had described the man in Diane Shaft's life as being 'odd in the head'. Aiden Brooks would certainly fit that description. DI Sally Speckle had a sudden wish that DS Andy Lukeson was with her. To hear what he thought of Aiden Brooks. To know if Brooks made Andy as uneasy as he was making her.

'And how might Mrs Staunton have passed over, Mr Brooks?'

'Violently. I know this because she's troubled, you see. I can sense her anger. She wasn't ready to cross over, Inspector. Such souls always leave behind an aura. I woke during the night and there it was, a kind of purple fog.'

Was Brooks a nutter? Or a killer, perhaps? Or a nutter and a killer?

'Cecily's earthly essence. Her energy. Hanging on here because it didn't want to go there, you see.' His chuckle was like rattling bones. 'And you think I'm barking mad, don't you?'

'I'll admit to being a little sceptical, Mr Brooks.'

'Just a little?' he scoffed. 'That is a pity. You must come to one of my seances and be convinced that there's much more to existence than the here and now.'

'You said that Cecily Staunton left this world violently?'

'Yes. Very violently, I feel.' He pulled his overcoat tighter round him and gave a little shiver. 'Cecily was murdered, Inspector.'

'When did you last see her, Mr Brooks?'

'I've told you, three days ago. I was supposed to see her yesterday. But a dear friend asked me to hold a seance. A couple of weeks ago her husband died suddenly — heart attack. She wanted to know from him if it was the argument they had had just before he popped off that had caused him to have his heart attack. Sadly, it was.'

'He told you this, did he?'

'Yes.'

'I see.'

'But you don't see, do you Inspector? You think that I'm a charlatan,' he stated petulantly, a sudden and nasty peevishness in his dark, marble eyes.

'I haven't got an opinion, Mr Brooks.'

'Liar!'

'I beg your pardon.'

'Of course you have an opinion,' Brooks snapped. 'I find that everyone does. So why should you be any different.'

Sally Speckle got an impression of a great repressed anger.

'We're not here to discuss my opinions, Mr Brooks,' Speckle said firmly. 'You've reported a woman missing. And I'm a police officer trying to help you.'

'Rubbish!'

A PC talking to the desk sergeant moved a little closer.

'OK, so you're a clairvoyant — '

'Yes.'

'So as a clairvoyant you should know where Cecily Staunton is?'

'Was.'

'I beg your pardon.'

'I said was. Cecily has been moved. But I think I can tell you where she was.' Aiden

Brooks closed his eyes and the colour drained away from his face with the intensity of his concentration. 'Her body was near water.'

'Her body?' Speckle pounced.

'Her body,' Brooks emphasised. 'I get a sense of flowing water. A stream, perhaps? No, a river! The flow of water is too strong to be a stream.' A pulse throbbed in his temple. 'Not far away. Maybe the river here in Loston?' His dark eyes popped open, making Sally Speckle flinch.

'Is there anything else you can tell us, Mr Brooks?' she asked, shaken.

He smirked smugly. 'What's this? A sudden conversion?' He sniffed the air. 'The central heating doesn't help, of course. But I'm picking up a dankness, a decay. Possibly a wood.'

'A wood near a river?'

'Yes.' He snorted. 'We're getting something of an audience, Inspector.'

Sally Speckle spun round to glare at the small gathering of plain-clothes and uniformed officers, looking on curiously, a gathering that broke up and returned to whatever they should be doing under her glare.

'I'm impressed, Inspector,' Aiden Brooks mocked. He laughed.

'Something amusing, Mr Brooks?' Speckle asked stiffly.

'Oh, please do not take offence,' Brooks said, as if he meant it. 'I'm not laughing at you. Oh, no. It's Roger's discomfiture at having had Cecily dumped on him again so soon after he had died to escape her attentions that I find droll. You see, I believe Roger Staunton didn't fall off that cliff. He jumped, rather than have to face Cecily again.'

He leaned close.

'You know, when Cecily and I were at it, sometimes I found Roger's anger more pleasurable than Cecily's body. Sensing his rage would make me all the more eager. I think I must have been a much better lover than he.'

'You don't seem very upset by — ?'

'Cecily being gone? A bit relieved, actually.'

'Why would that be, Mr Brooks?'

'In an unguarded moment I asked Cecily to marry me. It wouldn't have worked out. And if someone hadn't sent her to the Happy Hunting Ground . . . well, she might have sued me for breach of promise. Or is that done any more?'

'Just a moment.' Speckle went to the desk sergeant's phone to make a call to the mortuary. When she arrived back she said:

‘We’ll need you to identify a body we found near the river this morning, Mr Brooks.’

‘It’ll be Cecily all right,’ he said.

‘Do you know why she might have been also known as Diane Shaft, Mr Brooks?’ Speckle enquired.

He hunched his shoulders in response.

‘Does it surprise you that Cecily Staunton has already been reported missing as Diane Shaft?’

‘Cecily was the secretive type. Wouldn’t surprise me in the least if she had another life other than with me, Inspector. On reflection, I think that that was probably her attraction for me. Nothing as stimulating as intrigue, is there.’

The questions to be answered now were: Was Aiden Brooks a genuine clairvoyant? An exhibitionist crackpot who had learned of the murder? Perhaps he was one of the crowd who had gathered? Or was he Cecily Staunton’s killer playing some bizarre and sick game?

Whatever else Aiden Brooks might be, there was one thing he definitely was.

Weird.

3

When Sally Speckle entered the briefing room, DC Charlie Johnson looked like he was ready to commit murder himself. He was flanked by PC Brian Scuttle and WPCs Sue Blake and Anne Fenning. DC Helen Rochester was sitting off to one side, as if cast out from the group like a Biblical leper. The silence from what was normally a chatty group was intense.

'Sorry to have had to call you in, Charlie,' Speckle apologized, thinking that it was what might have been seen as high-handed attitude which had caused the obvious rift in team unity. 'But you'll understand why. With Andy Lukeson away on a course we're short-handed enough without being down one more.'

Her apology made not one whit of difference to the mood, and it slowly registered with Speckle that there was something other than having summoned Johnson back to duty that had precipitated the moody atmosphere.

'OK,' she said brusquely. 'What's the cold-shoulder treatment all about?'

Sue Blake and Anne Fenning avoided her

gaze, while DCs Charlie Johnson and Helen Rochester glared at each other combatively.

'Helen?'

Rochester was reluctant to get involved.

'Charlie, then?'

His response matched Rochester's.

Patience snapping, Speckle barked, 'Why do I get the feeling that I've gone from being a DI in Loston CID to being a bloody kindergarten teacher? Now,' her finger wagged between Rochester and Johnson, 'the problem here is obviously between you two. So, my office. Now! Well?' she demanded a moment later.

Rochester said, 'It's about me being the Acting DS, boss.'

'That's a problem?'

'Of course it's a problem.' Speckle directed her attention to Charlie Johnson. 'I'm the senior DC. If Andy Lukeson is missing, I should be his replacement.'

'Why is that, Charlie?' the DI asked.

'Because it's the system, ma'am. The way things are done. When the DS isn't around, the senior DC stands in as Acting DS. It's the way it's always been. Tradition, ma'am. You're not a . . . well not a — '

'Not a copper, as such, DC Johnson? One of the old school?' Charlie Johnson cringed. 'A 'graddie'?' That disparaging term to describe a copper with a university education.

'Or maybe a 'poshie' as DS George would have it.'

'With respect, ma'am,' Johnson said. 'You can't just ignore the . . . system.'

'As your DI, I am obliged to make the best use of available resources, and that means putting the right people in the right places to get the job done. And at this time, it is my judgement that DC Rochester is best suited to replace Andy Lukeson. You can accept, reject, or challenge that decision, DC Johnson. But until, and if, higher authority overrules my decision, it stands.'

'Then you leave me no option but to request a transfer to another DI, ma'am.'

'That will take time, DC Johnson. In the meantime, I expect you to be a full, contributing member of this team, and for you to carry out your duties to the full and without acrimony. Is that understood?'

'Ma'am.'

The atmosphere crackled.

Helen Rochester, clearly wishing that she could be anywhere else, offered, 'Look, if it will help, I'll step aside.'

'I don't want that,' Johnson stated.

'Neither do I,' Speckle added. She addressed Rochester: 'I made you Acting DS, and if you're not willing to accept my decision and judgement, Helen, then the same option as is open to DC Johnson is also open to you. We have a murder to solve. And I don't want this investigation jeopardized by squabbling between my officers.'

Sally Speckle wondered if she had taken too hard a stance. However, now that she had, relenting would only bring further dissention down the line which, in the long run, would make the team unmanageable and her authority untenable.

'I know that this might sound like horseshit right now, Charlie,' she said. 'But I reckon that the team will be all the poorer for your going.'

'You're right, boss. It does sound like horseshit,' he stated bluntly.

'Let me be perfectly clear,' Speckle's eyes flashed between Johnson and Rochester. 'This matter rests until our murderer is caught. Any argy-bargy, and I'll not hesitate to drop one or both of you from the team and implement disciplinary procedures if this investigation is in the least way compromised. Is *that* understood?'

Rochester and Johnson nodded.

After a difficult silence, Helen Rochester was first to speak. 'What's all this I'm hearing about a clairvoyant? Is he for real?'

'Frankly, I don't know what to make of Aiden Brooks,' Sally Speckle confessed.

'And he knew where the body was?' Charlie Johnson said. 'Near a river. Some place dank.'

The DI smiled. 'Nice to know that the Loston nick grapevine is in perfect working order.'

'A nutter looking for publicity?' Rochester speculated. 'They come out of the woodwork every time there's a murder.'

'He could also be a nutter and the killer looking for publicity,' Johnson said.

'I think it would be prudent to definitely consider both of those possibilities,' Speckle said.

* * *

When they returned to the briefing room, the other members of the team were edgy. While waiting for Speckle's return there had been the inevitable discussion about the merits or demerits of both Rochester and Johnson's positions — Brian Scuttle had been adamant that Speckle had called it right and that Helen Rochester was the better DC and therefore more deserving of being Andy Lukeson's temporary replacement, and his forceful promotion of that view had not been helpful. WPC Anne Fenning had charged Scuttle with bias in favour of his partner.

Sally Speckle was tempted to repeat her comments of a moment before about not tolerating any acrimony but she held back, hoping instead that once the murder investigation proper got going, the team's instinctive desire to bring Cecily Staunton's killer to justice would bond them. She could not help but wonder what Andy Lukeson would think. However, one thing she was certain of. If the investigation went belly up, it would be interpreted as a failure which would not have happened had Lukeson not been missing.

The cockup of a graddie. Or a poshie.

'Right,' she said, calling the briefing to order. 'Let's solve this murder. As of now, we haven't got a great deal to work with until we get full forensics and postmortem reports, but we can start with what we've got instead of sitting on our hands.'

'With the body lying in the open for a couple of days, trace evidence will be greatly reduced or damaged. We have a partial footprint found on a piece of cardboard, the pattern of which might prove to be helpful. On the other hand it might simply be the footprint of some innocent passer-by.

'The victim, though originally thought to be a woman called Diane Shaft, has now been positively identified as Cecily Staunton.'

‘How come Ruby Cox thought she was Diane Shaft, then?’ Rochester asked.

‘Maybe it’s the same woman that Brooks and Cox are talking about. One woman, two names.’ Speckle said.

‘Why?’ Johnson asked.

‘When we find that out, I reckon we’ll be a long way to catching her killer, Charlie. Any luck running Cox to ground?’ she enquired of Helen Rochester.

‘I’m on it,’ Anne Fenning said. ‘No form. Not under that name, anyway.’

‘The electoral register?’

‘Six Ruby Cox’s listed. Uniform are checking them out.’

‘Then let’s hope that Ruby Cox is her real name,’ WPC Sue Blake said. ‘Being a friend of Shaft or now correctly Staunton, they might both share Shaft’s fondness for multiple names.’

‘Good point, Sue,’ Speckle complimented the most junior member of the team. ‘Renault Meganes, Anne?’

WPC Anne Fenning opened her arms to indicate a long list.

‘*Red* Renault Meganes, then?’

Fenning closed her arms, but not by very much.

‘And the man waiting in the car for Cox?’ Speckle enquired, a touch exasperated.

'Anything on CCTV?'

'The camera outside the station that might have picked him up is waiting to be repaired,' Helen Rochester said. 'A drunk slung a rock at it the night before last.'

DI Sally Speckle hung her head.

'What about the clairvoyant of Loston?' Scuttle enquired with a scoff.

'Don't be such a cynic,' WPC Sue Blake rebuked him.

'You don't believe all that mumbo-jumbo, do you?' Scuttle asked Blake.

'I'm not sure. But I'm willing to keep an open mind, Brian.'

'Bloody hell! Believe in small green men from Mars as well, do you?'

'Closed minds lead to prejudice,' Blake flung back. 'That's how women were burned as witches because they simply had a black cat. And in some places people with epilepsy are regarded as being possessed.'

'Oh, I see. That fish bowl in your bedroom is not a fish bowl but a crystal ball, then?'

The unspoken question that shot to the forefront was: how the hell would Brian Scuttle know about the fishbowl in Sue Blake's bedroom? By Scuttle's and Blake's reaction, it was clear that the proverbial cat had been let out of the bag. It had been generally known about the nick that Scuttle's marriage was in trouble.

Was Sue Blake that trouble?

More importantly from DI Sally Speckle's perspective, if that were the case, how would it impact on the investigation? Feuding lovers would most definitely not help. So should she take both of them aside and have a quiet word? Were Scuttle's and Blake's personal lives any of her damn business to begin with? It was not like the 'good old days' before the mountain of red tape governing every aspect of working life, when a DI could take officers aside and knock heads together. Such an approach now could land one in all sorts of trouble. How would she react if she were Sue Blake? That was the best yardstick to judge by, and it did not take her long to come up with an answer. She'd be bloody furious if someone poked their nose, official or otherwise, into her personal life.

Speckle decided to wait and hope that the flash of angst between Brian Scuttle and Sue Blake had not been the opening salvo in an all-out war. And that her mounting problems would not keep mounting.

'The question that begs an answer,' the DI said, getting the briefing back on track, 'is whether Brooks has genuine clairvoyant powers, or if his clairvoyant insight is as bogus as Charlie Johnson's claim that Casanova has nothing on him.'

The laughter diverted attention away from Scuttle and Blake.

'Or did Brooks know where Cecily Staunton's body was because he left it there?'

'I'd say the latter,' WPC Anne Fenning opined.

'You spoke to him; what do you think?' WPC Sue Blake enquired of Speckle.

'Well, Brooks has a certain . . . aura,' she replied vaguely.

'Aura?' Johnson questioned.

'Presence.'

'You mean Brooks is weird.' Charlie Johnson said, making a statement rather than asking a question.

'People like him are a bit unusual.' All attention focused on WPC Sue Blake. 'Well, clairvoyants are not like you and me, are they?'

'Rubbish!' Scuttle barked, seeming intent on renewing hostilities.

Sally Speckle's worst fears were confirmed. She was angry. She had enough on her plate with DS Andy Lukeson off in Brighton, DC Charlie Johnson unhappy about not being Lukeson's replacement, and now the tribulations of an affair that had obviously lost its sheen to contend with. And, of course, the little matter of a murder to solve.

'There are unusual people in the world, Brian,' Fenning said, probably acting in support of another female doing battle with the male of the species. 'If there weren't, it would be a pretty glum old place, wouldn't it.'

Scuttle looked at Anne Fenning with scornful pity, which did not help.

'I agree with Anne.' That Charlie Johnson should, surprised everyone, not least of all Sally Speckle. 'When my mum passed away when I was just,' he held his hand palm down a couple of feet off the floor, 'so high, my dad went to a seance to ask Mum what he should do about selling up and moving nearer to her sister here in Loston. She had offered to help out with me, but Dad and my aunt didn't get on very well. Dad always swore that it was Mum's voice he heard, telling him to make the move.'

'Don't you see,' Scuttle argued. 'People who go to this kind of jiggery-pokery hear what they want to hear. They're preconditioned, aren't they.'

'My dad was a very down-to-earth Yorkshire man, not given to believing in anything until it was proven,' Johnson said.

Scuttle, made dogged now by his isolation, barked, 'I'm in a room with a crowd of nutters!'

Speckle stepped in as Sue Blake, Anne Fenning and Charlie Johnson jostled to be the first to respond. 'That'll do! This is not a forum to discuss the merits or demerits of things superstitious or supernatural.'

The reprimand had the effect of a cracking whip.

'We have a body. We know how this woman was murdered, by filling her air passages with glue, causing her to choke. But she was first stunned by a blow to the temple and was bound hand and foot. We have an identity. We know she was widow.'

'The Merry Widow, eh,' Scuttle snorted.

Speckle chose to ignore the jibe.

'We have a man who knew exactly where her body was, who claims that he knew because he's a clairvoyant. But this man was in a relationship with her that might have turned sour.

'The woman was expensively dressed; the exclusive, very exclusive, label on her clothes confirms this. So could she afford such clothing? Or if she could not afford to dress so chicly, then where did she get the money to dress so exclusively?

'And how was the victim previously identified as Diane Shaft, before her clairvoyant friend arrived on the scene? How did Ruby Cox know Cecily Staunton as Diane

Shaft? We need to find her to tell us why.

'Alec Balson reckons that there was no sexual assault, but the PM will tell either way. However, that does not mean that the murderer was not sexually motivated.'

'You mean the killer got his jollies by watching her die?'

'Succinctly, if ungraciously put,' Speckle told Scuttle.

'A spade's a spade, isn't it, boss.'

Speckle, who was known to be intolerant of wool-gatherers agreed, 'Indeed it is, Brian.'

'If he can only charge his battery by watching someone die, then that makes him a very dangerous animal,' Charlie Johnson observed. 'Because the next time he feels the urge, he'll have to kill another woman.'

'That is a very real danger, and a very good reason for finding the killer before that urge is upon him or her again,' Speckle agreed.

'Her?' Helen Rochester said.

'Women murder, too,' the DI said. 'And women kill other women for all sorts of reasons. So don't automatically assume that the killer is a man.'

'Why wasn't Brooks held for questioning?' Scuttle asked.

'On what grounds?'

'Suspicion of murder.'

'Aiden Brooks came in voluntarily to help

the police. Holding him on suspicion of murder, without the slightest proof would, I'm sure, be quickly set aside.'

'These clairvoyant powers are so much claptrap,' Scuttle said. 'Brooks knew where she was because he left her there after doing her in.'

'So, let's prove it, Brian!' Sally Speckle said. 'Without proof, the newspapers would have a field day at our expense, rattling on about police heavy-handedness.'

'The newspapers?' Johnson said. 'Why should we worry about what the newspapers would make of it?'

Johnson's question was indeed a very good question, and Sally Speckle wondered if she was (as she had promised herself that she never would) being sucked into the over-cautious approach of an officer whose decisions were more influenced by what the media would think and the ensuing publicity first, rather than victim and killer first. In fact, a member of the close-knit and inward-looking police establishment so intolerant of boat-rockers, that she had resolved not so long ago never to become.

Andy Lukeson (who had remained uninfluenced by the establishment; if he had not, he would have long ago been a DI if not a DCI, it was said) had warned her early on when she had expressed her determination to always put the investigation first, of the ease with which one could be induced or seduced into 'the system'.

'Keeping your nose clean at all costs creeps up on you,' he had said, over a pint in the Plodders Well (officially the King's Head, but called the Plodders Well because of it's closeness to the Loston nick and its numerous police clientele). 'You always need to be on your guard against that, Sally.'

She now had to be careful not to over-react, and go off half-cocked from some misguided sense of endorsing her stated view that newspapers should never be allowed to decide on what direction an investigation would take. Because on this occasion she was sure that pulling Aiden Brooks in for questioning would not (as matters stood and until there was more definite evidence of his involvement in Cecily Staunton's murder, other than his self-proclained clairvoyant knowledge) warrant his detention. Because, equally, if Brooks was pulled in, the *Echo* would be quick to report that a man was helping the police with their inquiries, and the headlines would be all the bigger and more lurid (the *Loston Echo*, once an informative broadsheet was now a tabloid and owned by a group that sold newspapers on sensationalism and free CDs of has-been pop groups) because of Aiden Brooks claim to be a pyschic. That would start a circus round the investigation, and she believed that police work was best done quietly and unobstrusively.

'To formally question Brooks right now, we would need more than we have, Charlie,' Sally Speckle said.

Johnson was clearly displeased by her answer, and also obviously of the opinion that she was thinking primarily of the bad PR that might ensue, and playing it safe the way senior officers did — particularly those who were just beginning to climb the greasy pole of promotion. It was a common view held by junior officers of senior officers and was sometimes correct, but not always. She had also to take into account Johnson's disgruntlement at being, as he would see it, passed over.

DC Charlie Johnson found an ally, surprisingly so from Speckle's point of view, in WPC Anne Fenning. 'What if Brooks is a nutter, boss? And we let him hang round out there to top another woman?'

What if indeed, Speckle thought.

'Might be safer to have Brooks in for questioning,' Acting DS Helen Rochester joined in. 'At least then, if the shit hits the fan, we'll have been seen to have done something.'

Unsettled by Rochester's lack of support, Speckle said, 'This is not a bloody democracy! I'm in charge of the investigation, so I call the shots.'

It was an uncharacteristic outburst that did nothing at all to bond the team. And she was pretty sure that when the acrimonious nature of the exchanges in general reached Chief Superintendent Doyle's ears (which they inevitably would through a grapevine that M15 would give their eye teeth for) he would ask if she needed Andy Lukeson to be on hand. Or perhaps he would not bother asking and simply order Lukeson back. And were Doyle to do that, it would wipe out all the progress she had made in being accepted as a DI (by right rather than by virtue of her university education and entrance to the force by the graduate entrance programme) by her more traditionally promoted colleagues.

She was under no illusions. There were still many skulking in the wings to say: I told you so. And although she was on her third murder (the previous two successfully concluded), she knew there were some who felt that her success had more to do with Andy Lukeson than any deductive brilliance on her part. Though she missed his counsel and company, this was her first murder investigation without him, and were she to be successful, could there be any doubt left that she held her rank by right rather than patronage?

She welcomed the opportunity to prove that she was a good copper in her own right.

'Helen will give you your assignments.' Sally Speckle drifted past PC Brian Scuttle and said in an aside. 'My office in ten minutes. Bring Sue.' A moment later Scuttle and Blake arrived in her office, and without any attempt at sublety the DI stated: 'Sort out whatever is going on between you two. And the sooner the better.'

4

Shadows was Loston's most exclusive and upmarket boutique, the place where the richest, not necessarily the best women in Loston shopped when they were caught for time and could not fly to Milan or New York or Paris, of course, and from where Cecily Staunton's clothing had come. The lighting was soft. The carpet luxurious. The music was Chopin, but Speckle could not pin the piece down. Her brother Simon, who had taught her everything she knew about classical music, would have had the answer instantly. Chopin had been his favourite composer; hers was Mozart. Whenever she heard Chopin, the music always brought memories of her gentle gay brother who had died of Aids.

'Can I help, Madame?'

The woman who had appeared magically by her side was soft spoken and wore an exquisitely cut dark suit with just a suggestion of maleness to the collar that would not have appealed to Sally Speckle. On observing Speckle's off-the-peg outfit which even looked the worse for wear, the woman's tone became less welcoming, having obviously reached the conclusion that Speckle was not 'Shadows' people.

Her next remark confirmed this.

'If you're collecting for something, it's our policy not to encourage — '

'Police,' Speckle interjected and, glancing at the name tag, added, 'Ms Proudfoot.'

Agnes Proudfoot would have staggered, if such had been permitted in Shadows. Instead, she sniffed the air as if someone had been terribly rude.

'DI Sally Speckle.'

Speckle flashed her warrant card. The woman waved her fingers above her head as if she were swatting imaginary midges. The peculiar gesture was interpreted as a distress signal and another woman, who was reasonably well dressed but not in the Shadows league, came forward wearing a tag that simply said security.

'The police,' Ms Proudfoot said, as if not quite believing what was happening. 'Here. In Shadows.'

'What do you want?' the woman who had been summoned enquired of Speckle, in a manner that would have earned a Nazi death camp guard brownie points.

'Information. Isn't that what the police always want?'

'Information about what?'

'One of your customers.'

'A customer of Shadows involved with the police,' exclaimed Agnes Proudfoot in a flutter. If it was Victorian times she might have been described as having an attack of the vapours. 'You must be mistaken, Inspector.'

'A woman wearing clothes with this boutique's label on them has been found murdered. One must assume she's a customer until finding otherwise, Ms Proudfoot.'

'Might I suggest, Inspector, that this woman did not come by the clothes she was wearing by being a customer of Shadows, but rather by some other means, probably nefarious in nature.'

'I'd like to check your records,' Speckle said.

'Our records are most confidential!'

'This is a murder investigation,' Speckle said, in a no-nonsense fashion. 'Nothing is confidential.'

'Still, I'm not sure that I can disclose any det— '

'I can get a search warrant and come back with uniformed officers,' Speckle said.

Ms Proudfoot went rigid. 'Uniformed officers!' She looked about the quiet environs of Shadows and paled at the image her mind presented to her of plodders good and true traipsing round. 'Dear me, that would never do.'

'I have a murder to solve,' Speckle said sternly. 'And I mean to have any details that you might have on your records by cooperation or sanction, Ms Proudfoot. The choice is entirely yours.'

The security officer looked to Agnes Proudfoot for guidance.

'Oh, very well. If you would come along to my office. Was this purchase recent?'

'I think so. Her clothes were new.'

'That really tells us nothing.' Ms Proudfoot led the way to a recessed mahogany door to the left of the entrance. 'You see, Shadows garments, being the finest there are, can look new long after they have been purchased. We pride ourselves on that. Do you have a name for this woman, Inspector?'

'Cecily Staunton, I believe.'

'Would that be Mrs, Miss or Ms?'

'How many Stauntons do you have on your books?'

'We like to be precise,' the woman replied aloofly. 'Saves valuable time.' She said 'valuable time' in a manner which she considered a police officer incapable of understanding, raising Sally Speckle's hackles.

Once through the door, the glitz of Shadows vanished. The corridor and rooms off it were littered with empty boxes and all the detritus one might find lying around in one of those awful and to be despised high street trader's stores, flogging Asian mass-produced clothing which Shadows customers would not be caught dead in.

Disappointment was heaped on disillusionment.

Agnes Proudfoot's office was not the plush-scented oasis that Sally Speckle had imagined it would be. In fact, it was not much bigger than a shoebox and smelled of egg sandwiches. This conclusion was not down to Holmesian deduction on Speckle's part, but came from the experience of many evenings she had spent with her gran after school doing chores, a gran who was addicted to egg sandwiches, the smell of which became embedded in Sally Speckle's nostrils to be automatically ressurected whenever she came within the vicinity of an egg sandwich.

'Now — '

The woman went to one of three filing cabinets that took up most of the floor space, opened the middle one and rifled through its contents.

'You're sure that the dead woman's name is Staunton, are you?' she asked impatiently. 'Because we don't appear to have any Staunton on our accounts records.'

'Perhaps she wasn't a customer as such,' Speckle suggested.

'I'm not sure I know what you mean.' Then shocked: 'You mean a cash customer? A casual customer?' It was as if Speckle had slapped her across the face. 'Oh, dear me no. Shadows doesn't deal in cash, Inspector. Everything is charged.'

'So if someone walked in off the street.' Proudfoot was pained. 'Cash in hand.' Her pain increased tenfold. 'You'd tell her be on her way, would you?'

'Well, not in any brash sort of manner, of course. Our staff are trained to discreetly suggest that madame might prefer to frequent a lesser establishment than Shadows.'

'And if this person did not understand or accept your discreet suggestion?'

'We would unfortunately have to be more direct. We would ask security to show the woman off the premises.'

When it was obvious that Sally Speckle thought poorly of the boutique's policy of shopping apartheid, the woman rushed on. 'You must understand our trading position, Inspector. Shadows is built on exclusivity. Were we to lose our prestige, we would most certainly lose our customers. I'll check again.' She moved to the other filing cabinets. 'Perhaps the account has been misplaced.

These things happen.'

'Even in a bastion of exclusivity and correctness like Shadows,' Speckle intoned sarcastically.

Agnes Proudfoot, nose out of joint, searched all three filing cabinets and came up with the same answer. Shadows had no account for a customer by the name of Staunton. 'You're absolutely certain that the label on her clothes was ours, are you, Inspector?'

'Yes.'

Suddenly alarmed, Ms Proudfoot fretted, 'Oh, dear me. I do hope our garments are not being pirated. Or perhaps these were clothes passed on by one of our ladies,' she contemplated, the possibility giving her some comfort. And, warming to the idea: 'Many of Shadows clients are of a charitable nature, you see, who might pass on clothes to a charity, or perhaps a relative in less favourable circumstances.'

'It's a possibility, I suppose,' Speckle conceded.

'Sorry, I can't be of more help.'

'Thanks for taking the time, Ms Proudfoot. One more thing — ' Speckle produced a photograph of the dead woman. 'Do you know this woman?'

'No. The murdered woman?'

'Yes.'

'How horrible.'

'Indeed.' Speckle proffered the photograph again. 'You're sure?'

'Do come back it we can help in any way, Inspector.'

It was an invitation that was as genuine as a politician's promises at election time.

Sally Speckle was being shown out by a much relieved Agnes Proudfoot, who was anxious to hurry her along as discreetly as possible, when the DI paused. 'Do you have a client by the name of Diane Shaft, Ms Proudfoot?'

The question pulverized Proudfoot. 'Yes,' she replied quietly. 'We do.'

'And you're sure that it's not the woman in the photograph?'

'I can't say, Inspector.'

'Can't say?'

Acutely conscious of several women who were taking a keen interest in Ms Proudfoot's visitor, women who obviously had a herd instinct and recognized Sally Speckle as being outside of the herd, Agnes Proudfoot waved her hand in the general direction of the door from which they had just come.

'Perhaps — '

'Of course,' Speckle readily agreed.

Once back inside in the cluttered hall,

Proudfoot said, 'Ms Shaft is a customer of Shadows, yes. But we've never seen her.'

'Never seen her?'

'No. Oh dear, this is rather difficult. You see, all of Ms Shaft's clothes are bought for her and then sent round.'

'Bought for her?'

'Yes. By a gentleman.'

Plainly, all of Shadows customers may not have the pedigree they would have one believe their clients had.

'And this *gentleman's* name?'

'A Mr Rupert Fox.'

'Has Mr Fox been in recently?'

'Oh, Mr Fox never comes in. He gives us the ladies' sizes and leaves it to us to choose for him. And he always seems quite pleased with our choice. Happily so.'

'Ladies? Plural?'

'Yes.'

'How many ladies do you kit out for Mr Fox?'

'Kit out?' Agnes Proudfoot intoned indignantly. 'Shadows doesn't *kit out*, Inspector.'

'How many,' Speckle asked sharply, impatient with Proudfoot's antics.

'Ten.'

'His life must be exhausting.'

'Oh, it's not like that at all. I believe that Mr Fox runs a very exclusive escort agency.

Oh, not the lower end of the market kind of agency. Function escorts, that kind of thing,' she hastened to add. 'I mean he would hardly be coming to Shadows if . . . Well, you understand, I'm sure. And, of course, Mr Fox would not be involved in any — ' Agnes Proudfoot was floundering.

'Lower end of the market stuff?' Speckle suggested.

Proudfoot sagged.

'So, Fox orders and you deliver. Where to, Miss Proudfoot?'

'This is most distressing, Inspector,' Proudfoot pleaded.

'Where to?'

'Suite 306. The Oasis Hotel in Brigham,' she said resignedly.

'*Suite* 306?'

'There aren't any rooms in the Oasis, Inspector,' Agnes Proudfoot intoned haughtily. 'Only suites.'

Sally Speckle knew of the Oasis in the way that those who could never afford to be a guest there did. Owned by an Arab sheik, the Oasis was the essence in luxury and private living — very private living. It was an oddity in Brigham in the sense that Brigham would be the last place one would expect to find a hotel like the Oasis. And the only reason that it was there was that the sheik who had it built had passed through Brigham and for some inexplicable reason had liked the place. However, on his frequent return visits, he would need a suitable abode and the Oasis was it. To call the Oasis a hotel was a bit of a misnomer. It had all the appearance of a hotel, but its guests were permanent and strictly *rich list* patrons and obviously a pimp or two, as Sally Speckle was sure Mr Fox was. A place like the Oasis was a perfect hidey-hole for the less socially desirable and the downright criminal. Because Speckle doubted if there was a senior police officer who would not think of his future and his pension before raiding the place.

A phone call from an irate guest could end both.

'Is Fox English?' Speckle enquired.

'Yes. Very English.'

'When you say *very* English, do you mean aristocratic?'

'Possibly.'

'Or a very good actor, perhaps?'

Agnes Proudfoot was pained.

'You won't bother him at his hotel, will you?' she worried. 'I do hope we won't lose Mr Fox's custom, Inspector. It is quite considerable.'

'We'll be as discreet as possible,' Speckle reassured Agnes Proudfoot, who wasn't at all convinced. Speckle was leaving when a thought came to mind that was to have Ms Proudfoot in a panic when she asked, 'Have you ever heard of a woman called Ruby Cox, Ms Proudfoot?'

Speckle had to grab Proudfoot's arm as she wobbled on her feet. It was very plain that indeed she had heard of Ruby Cox.

'Another of Mr Fox's *ladies*, is she?'

5

On leaving Shadows, Speckle phoned Helen Rochester. 'Meet me at Aiden Brooks's house in Connoston Road.' She broke the connection and turned to go to her car, her much abused Punto, and groaned on seeing a traffic warden putting a parking ticket under her windscreen wiper. 'Heh,' she called out, as he strolled away, looking for his next victim. The traffic warden, none too pleased with Speckle's summons and ready to refuse all pleas, cast an *I'm not for turning* look her way. 'I'm a police officer,' Speckle informed him.

'Oh, yes,' the warden scoffed. 'And I could say that I'm Santa Claus.'

'You're too bloody skinny, mate,' Speckle said.

She took the ticket from the windscreen and offered it back. The traffic warden looked at her as if she had taken leave of her senses. Speckle showed him her warrant card.

'Being a DI doesn't give you the right to park illegally,' he said, and looking at the way the back of the Punto was over the white line of the parking area, he added, 'And dangerously, in my opinion, Inspector.'

'I'm investigating a murder,' Speckle said. 'Impeding me will bring a ton of grief on your head. Is that what you want?'

Plainly, it was not what the traffic warden wanted. She offered him back the parking ticket again.

'How the hell am I supposed to know who's a copper or not,' he grumbled. He had a point, of course. 'You lot should be upholding the law. Not breaking it.' The warden walked off grumbling, looking for some unfortunate driver he could vent his anger on which, by his grin, he found further along the street.

Speckle was getting into the Punto when she caught a glimpse of a woman rounding the corner on the opposite side of the street. She was about to hail Margaret Cranton, Sergeant Jerry Cranton's wife, when a passing bus cut off her view, and by the time the bus had passed she was gone. If she had time, she would have gone after Margaret Cranton. As a rookie she had stayed with the Crantons for a couple of weeks while she sought more permanent accomodation, and they could not have been kinder to her. She had come to know Margaret even better than Jerry, having long chats when Jerry was locked away in his darkroom developing yet another batch of photographs.

'I keep telling him that he'll go blind if he spends every spare minute looking through a camera,' Margaret would say. 'Sometimes I wish he'd be like other men and watch football.'

'I've seen some of his photographs,' Speckle had said. 'He's quite good.'

'I suppose,' Margaret Cranton had said despondently. 'And I suppose I might be kind of unusual as wives go.' She continued, more upbeat. 'Now if I was a football or a golf widow, I'd be pretty much part of the common herd, wouldn't I.'

As Sally Speckle pulled out into traffic a male driver was taking the traffic warden to task. He might as well have been a Christian pleading for mercy from Caligula, Speckle thought.

* * *

'Must have a couple of quid in his sock,' was Helen Rochester's observation ten minutes later when Speckle linked up with her outside Aiden Brooks's house in Connoston Road, one of Loston's up-market areas.

The house was Victorian, but had been added to, making it a very impressive house indeed. The additions blended perfectly with the original structure, obviously using materials and building skills proper to the era, the result being that as it stood the house in its entirety looked every inch authentic, and it would be only on a very keen inspection that the slight differences between the original and the added could be seen, and only then with a practiced eye.

The gardens were equally impressive, sweeping in a half circle round the house, home to a spectacular variety of flowers, trees, plants and shrubs.

'I bet each blade of grass is precisely the same length,' Rochester said, as they approached the front door.

'Wouldn't surprise me one little bit,' Speckle agreed.

'A polished brass bell pull,' Rochester said. 'Like in those period series on telly. Very law-dee-daw.'

'Well, pull it then,' Speckle said.

A moment later a woman appeared, somewhat frustrated, brushing back from her face wisps of fair hair that had escaped from a bun. The whirr of a vacuum cleaner and the duster in her hand were evidence that she was not the lady of the house.

'Yes?' she enquired curtly.

'DI Sally Speckle and DS Helen Rochester to see Mr Brooks,' Speckle said.

'Who?'

'Mr Aiden Brooks,' Speckle said.

'Don't know any Aiden Brooks,' the woman said.

'Well, this is the address he gave us only this morning,' Speckle said, feeling a sense of foreboding.

'That so.' The woman laughed. 'Then your Mr Brooks has put one over on you, ain't he.'

'Could we the speak to the owner, then?' Speckle asked.

'Off in Barbados. Got a gaff over there. Nice for some, ain't it. When the weather here ain't that good, off he pops to the sun.' With a nod she indicated the interior of the house. 'Don't know why he bothers. The place ain't never dirty. Lives on his own, does Mr Samuels.'

'Is there a photograph of Mr Samuels in the house you can show us?' the DI asked.

'Must be a dozen at least. All needin' dustin'.'

'Could we see one?'

'Yeah. Don't see why not. There's one right here in the hall.' Leaving the front door open, the woman went and fetched a silver-framed photograph from the hall table, came back and handed it to Speckle. 'That's him standin' 'longside his yacht. Nice work if you can get it, eh.'

On seeing the photograph of a fit but elderly man, Speckle exchanged a hopeless glance with Helen Rochester.

'Maybe we got the number of the house wrong,' Rochester said, and asked the cleaning woman, 'Is there a Brooks living anywhere on the road?'

'Oh, I wouldn't know nothin' about that. I clean for Mr Samuels and Ms Matterson,' she leaned out the door and pointed. 'Third house along,' she said. 'Don't know nothin' about no one else.'

'Do you know how long Ms Matterson has been a resident here?' Rochester asked.

'Oh, yonks. Ever since she was a kid. Grew up in the Laurels, that's the name of the house. Been there ever since. Nice woman, is Ms Matterson.'

The way she said, '*Nice woman, Ms Matterson*,' left no doubt that the same compliment could not be paid to Samuels.

'Thank you.'

'Heh,' the cleaning woman said, as they left, second guessing Speckle and Rochester's thoughts. 'Mebbe, Ms Matterson might know this bloke Brooks.'

'Good idea,' Speckle said.

'Yeah, it was, wasn't it,' the cleaner said, quite chuffed. 'Done somethin' wrong has he, this fella Brooks?'

Speckle and Rochester did not reply.

'Charmed, I'm sure,' the woman said.

Speckle and Rochester winced at the slam of the front door.

'Proof positive, I think,' Rochester said. 'That the Victorians built sound houses.' And as they walked to the Matterson house, 'Why do you reckon Brooks gave us a wrong address?'

'Maybe he had second thoughts about having reported Cecily Staunton missing,' Speckle proposed. 'Saw a whole pile of trouble coming his way and hoped that he could drop out of sight by giving us a false address.'

'Get away,' Helen Rochester said, pulling a mock shocked face. 'Diddle Loston's finest.' And on a more serious note: 'Brooks can't have believed that when we began turning stones that we wouldn't find him anyway.'

'True,' Speckle conceded. 'But panic and reason aren't bedfellows, Helen. And the innocent sometimes, due to panic, react as if they are guilty.'

'Do you think Brooks is guilty?'

Sally Speckle smiled. 'You have a disturbing way of cutting to the chase, Sergeant.'

'Do you?' Rochester pressed.

'Let's say that the jury is out yet.'

'A typical DI cop-out,' Helen Rochester

said good humouredly.

The Laurels, though not as impressive as the Samuels' house, was not to be sneezed at. But it was beginning to show some frayed edges, and the gardens were not as pristine as its near neighbour. Only an area close to the house was being tended to, and Speckle reckoned that the fencing that divided the garden was a shield to hide the garden's decrepitude beyond that point, evident in the long stalks of wild and unplanned growth poking up over the top of the fence.

The front door opened before they reached it.

'What do you want?' a frail, elderly woman, presumably Ms Matterson, enquired of Speckle and Rochester. 'Didn't you see the sign on the gate warning against tresspass?'

They had seen the sign, and also a more worrying, BEWARE OF DOG addendum. But thankfully there was no dog in sight — yet. However, Speckle and Rochester remained ready to flee should a snarling canine rush from the rear of the house.

'The police can be here very quickly,' the frightened Ms Matterson said, in a tone of voice that held more hope than certainty of her claim being proved should it be acted on.

'We *are* the police,' DI Sally Speckle said. 'Ms Matterson, is it?'

She did not confirm her identity, but asked suspicously, 'The police you say? I'm not fooled easily, you know.'

'We really are police officers, Ms Matterson,' Speckle reassured the frightened woman. She held out her warrant card which Ms Matterson examined carefully.

'Detective Inspector — ' She screwed up her china-blue eyes, alive with an undiminished intelligence, 'Speckle, is it?'

'Yes.'

'I knew a Margery Speckle once. Any relation?'

'I don't think so.'

'Unusual name. Not a very pretty one though, is it,' she added with blunt honesty. 'Oh, dear,' the elderly woman fretted. 'I didn't mean to — '

'We have to take what we get, don't we, Ms Matterson,' the DI said genially, much to Ms Matterson's relief. 'And my colleague is Acting Detective Sergeant Helen Rochester.'

'Never knew anyone by that name. Those things,' she waved a bony finger at the warrant card, 'can be quite easily forged.'

'Would you care to phone Loston CID to verify our identity, while we wait here.'

'Don't have the phone number, do I.'

'I'll give you the number, Ms Matterson,' Speckle said, by now her patience with the elderly lady's obstinancy wearing a little thin.

'What good would that do? You could have mugged the real officers and stolen their identity. Or you could be giving me the number of an accomplice waiting for the call.'

'I blame it all on telly,' Helen Rochester mumbled behind Speckle.

'We've just left the Samuels house having spoken to the cleaning lady — '

'Mrs Booth.'

'Yes.'

Speckle had almost said that she did not know the cleaner's name, but that would have started another bout of suspicion.

'Good woman, Mrs Booth. Does her work conscientiously. What did you want at the Samuels house? Hasn't been broken into, has he? He's all right, isn't he?'

'Perfectly fine,' Speckle reassured Ms Matterson.

'What do you want with me, Inspector? I have paid my television licence, you know.'

'I'm sure you have, Ms Matterson. May we come in?'

'No. Like I said you might have — '

'I understand,' Speckle interjected. 'We were actually looking for a man by the name of Brooks who gave us Mr Samuels' address, obviously in error, and Mrs Booth said — '

'Brooks, did you say?'

'Yes.'

'Harold, would it be?'

'No. A Mr Aiden Brooks.'

'Oh, dear. No good, that one. Mischief was his middle name. Gone. Sold up a couple of years ago. Soon after Elizabeth Brooks died, that would be Harold's wife. Nice man, Harold. A kind man. Never did understand how he had such a bad apple for a son.'

'Bad apple?' Helen Rochester prompted.

'I'd have thought she was dumb,' she said to Speckle. Ms Matterson cast a cold eye over Rochester. 'If I hadn't heard her comment about blaming it all on the telly.'

Helen Rochester winced.

Ms Matterson laughed mischievously. 'That rocked your boat, didn't it, young lady. Thought old and deaf went together, didn't you.'

'Sorry,' Rochester apologized.

'Don't be.' Then, sadly, 'It's the first time I've laughed in a long time.' Brightening, 'Bad apple. Well, there was something wrong with Aiden Brooks.'

'Something wrong?' Speckle prompted.

'Sensed it,' Ms Matterson said. 'The way he'd creep up on one. And the way he'd look at you. I don't think evil would be a description too far off the mark. Always gave me the shivers. I was glad when Harold sold up. Though I miss his neighbourliness.' Her brow furrowed. 'Why would Aiden Brooks give you this address?'

Why indeed?

'Oh, I'm sure it's a genuine mistake on Mr Brooks' part, Ms Matterson.'

'In a pig's eye! You don't believe that for a second, Inspector.'

'Do you know where we might find Aiden Brooks now, Ms Matterson?'

'Under some rock or other, I shouldn't wonder.'

'And Mr Harold Brooks?'

'Lives with his sister in Gregory Street. Number 6, I think.'

'And his son doesn't live with him?'

'Harold's sister, Aiden Brooks's aunt, wouldn't have him inside the front door Harold told me on a visit, some time ago now. Can't say that I blame her.'

'What did Aiden Brooks do to deserve being such an outcast, Ms Matterson?' Rochester asked.

The old lady leaned towards Speckle and Rochester. 'Murdered his sister, for one thing. Evelyn was her name. A sweet girl.'

'When was this?' Speckle asked, stunned by the revelation.

'Oh, must be all of thirty years ago now. They were playing in the garden. They had a small swimming pool back then which

Samuels had filled in. Evelyn was in the pool. They said she drowned. An accident they said. But Elizabeth, Aiden's tortured mother, knew different.

'Before she died, when I went to see her in the hospice, Elizabeth told me about what she had seen that day. She had left the garden and had gone upstairs to the bathroom, but had been diverted to a bedroom overlooking the garden. A stiffish breeze had blown up so she went into the bedroom to close an open window. She happened to look out on the garden and she saw Aiden standing over Evelyn in the pool. Protectively, she thought. Until he bent down and pushed her under the water.

'Horrified, Elizabeth lost precious seconds before she ran back downstairs and out to the garden. But by then it was too late. She found Aiden in a kind of trance, looking down at Evelyn. And then he began to laugh.

'Elizabeth told me that she would never forget that laugh. That from that moment on, it was forever inside her head. Cruel and evil, she said it was. She died a couple of hours after confiding in me. And I lost a good friend.'

'Perhaps the palliative medication which Mrs Brooks would have been taking made her — '

'Imagine things, Inspector?' Ms Matterson shook her head adamantly. 'Elizabeth was perfectly lucid. I think she just had to talk to someone. She didn't want to leave this world without passing on her awful secret. She made me promise not to tell Harold. Said that it would break him.'

'At the time, did Mrs Brooks not tell the police what she had seen?' Helen Rochester asked.

'No. So you musn't either.' Ms Matterson's hand shot to her mouth. 'Oh, dear. Silly me. You are the police. I've never told the police about what Elizabeth told me. It was a secret, you see. And if I told the police Harold would have been bound to find out, wouldn't he. You'd want to question him, I expect.'

'Do you know what explanation Elizabeth Brooks gave to the police at the time?' Speckle enquired.

'That Evelyn had fainted. She had a history of fainting. Some medical condition she had been born with. So it was a history that Elizabeth very cleverly used. She said that she had gone inside the house and had seen Evelyn fall into the pool from the bedroom window, and by the time she got to Evelyn she had drowned.'

'And Aiden Brooks. Did the police question him?'

'Elizabeth told them that he was not in the garden. That after lunch he got a tummy upset and she had put him to bed to rest.'

'And Harold Brooks?'

'He was at work. And he accepted Elizabeth's account of what had happened. He had no reason to question it. Harold trusted Elizabeth explicitly.'

'Well, thank you, Ms Matterson.'

Sally Speckle turned to leave.

'What will you do about all of this?'

'It's all happened a very long time ago,' Speckle said non-committedly. 'Now, do you know where we might find Aiden Brooks, Ms Matterson?'

'No. I'm just glad that he's gone from here.'

'Well, thank you, Ms Matterson. You've been most helpful.'

'Aren't you coming in? Police officers always want to come in.'

Sally Speckle recognized the eldery woman's need for company, but regrettably, being in the middle of a murder inquiry, she did not have the time to socialize.

'We're rather pushed for time, Ms Matterson. But perhaps I could call round at another time for a chat.'

Ms Matterson's considerable pride took over. 'Oh, no, Inspector. I'm much too busy to sit around chatting idly.'

The front door closed.

Helen Rochester's observation that Ms Matterson 'just wanted the company', did nothing to ease Sally Speckle's conscience. Perhaps, she thought, that when the case was over she would risk coming round anyway.

'Funny old business with Evelyn Brooks,' Rochester said, as they walked back to Speckle's Punto parked outside the Samuels house. 'Our colleagues of the time seemed very trusting, you reckon?'

'Thirty years ago was a different country, wasn't it.'

'And now?'

'What realistic chance would we have of ever charging Aiden Brooks with his sister's murder. Any evidence would long since be gone, and all we'd have would be a very elderly woman's story about a heavily sedated dying woman who told her this fantastic story about a murder in her back garden thirty years ago. I think the Crown Prosecution Service would laugh us out of the room, don't you.'

Rochester's mobile rang.

'Helen.' It was WPC Anne Fenning. 'I've got a Freddie Knott on to me. He wants to know if you've found his stolen BMW?'

Rochester groaned. Knott had been on

every day, sometimes two or three times a day, since his motor had been stolen, not that she blamed him. If she had had a top-of-the-range BMW nicked, she'd want it back too.

'Tell him that the invstigation is progressing.'

'I don't know if he'll accept that as an answer.'

'It's what I tell him. And there really is no other answer, until we crack the ring involved. Yeah, she's here.'

Rochester handed her mobile to Speckle.

'What is it, Anne?'

'It's about this woman who called herself Ruby Cox — '

'What about her?'

'It's this picture from the CCTV in the reception area. I've seen her before.'

'Where?'

'It's a bit awkward, boss.'

'Why's that?'

'Well, the person I saw her with is Jerry Cranton.'

6

Gregory Street seemed determined to hold on to its former glory for as long as it could, but the slow unstoppable rot was beyond redemption. The house whose brass knocker DC Charlie Johnson was hammering on was still in relatively good condition compared to its near neighbours, but it too, without attention, would follow the same pattern of decay.

'Miss Brooks?'

Charlotte Brooks, Harold Brooks's sister had, DC Charlie Johnson reckoned, the sour, discontented look of a woman who was a spinster but who had never planned on being one and, now that all hope of marriage had faded, had become embittered with a lot she would never have chosen had fate been kinder to her. When she opened the front door, she was rubbing an oily gel into her hands that smelled of dank undergrowth, evidence of its herbal properties. Seeing the tell-tale nodules of arthritis on Charlotte Brooks's hands, which would soon completely deform them, it was probable that the foul-smelling gel was a treatment for the arthritis. Johnson thought that before the crippling disease had struck, Charlotte Brooks's now twisted hands had been beautifully formed.

Johnson had a sense of having seen Charlotte Brooks somewhere before.

There was a crash from inside the house. Charlotte Brooks turned round to rebuke the black and white cat who was on the hall table and had sent a figurine crashing to the floor. 'My brother will have cats about the place breaking things,' she complained. 'Yes,' she confirmed curtly, her face filling with pain on striking a particularly inflamed spot on her hands, 'I'm Charlotte Brooks.'

'DC Charlie Johnson,' he introduced himself.

'What's that six-foot-three long string of misery got up to now?' Charlotte Brooks asked.

'Beg your pardon?'

'Aiden, of course. I suppose you'd better come in, hadn't you.'

Though Charlie Johnson had come to speak to Harold Brooks, Aiden's father, he now left Charlotte Brooks under the impression that it was Aiden he had come to see, in the hope that a fuller picture of Aiden Brooks and the kind of man he was would emerge.

'It's not about that incident last Saturday, is it?'

Johnson made no denial, hoping that his

silence would be taken as a positive by Charlotte Brooks, and it was.

'I thought charges weren't to be pressed?'

Johnson gave a non-committal shrug.

'Such a fuss about whether the bananas should be weighed imperially or metrically. Aiden, of course, was wrong to try and throttle the stallholder, but surely there's wrong also on the stallholder's part. It was just a silly little episode. I understood that it had all been settled and the police weren't taking action. And now — '

'Easily upset, is he, Aiden Brooks?' Johnson asked.

'He can be. Well, he can have a temper. My nephew is a paranoid schizophrenic, Constable. If he's taking his medication, he can be quite stable. But he doesn't always take his medication, you see. He goes through periods of rebellion when he won't listen to anyone and he can be very unpredictable then.

'His dark moods phase, Harold, his father, calls it. I'm less of a romantic and calls it what it is — his lunatic period. Often goes completely blank and can't remember what he's done. And when he realizes what he has done, he comes up with a fictionalized account of the episode that, believe me, can be utterly convincing.'

'Is Aiden Brooks violent during these moods?'

'A bit threatening. When he goes off the deep end, Harold packs him off of to The Cedars.'

'The private clinic?'

'Clinic? A euphemism for an asylum, Constable. There, they calm Aiden down and get him back on his medication. Then, until the next time he decides to quit his medication, he can be as normal as you and I.

'Whatever normality is. I suppose we all have a little madness in us, don't you agree?'

'I suppose.'

'Harold pays the bills. More fool he. I've told him to let Aiden experience the NHS and he wouldn't be so ready to give up his medication. Aiden will bleed his father dry of every penny if he's not more firm with him. But Harold worries that when he's no longer around, Aiden won't be able to survive. Utter rot, of course. Like the proverbial cat, Aiden always lands on his feet.'

Treading on eggshells, Johnson said, 'A difficult situation, not knowing when a mood might be triggered or what by.'

'Usually when the voices come. Particularly his dead sister's voice. Evelyn died when they were children. She drowned. Aiden was there, and I think he blames himself for not having done anything. But they were both children.'

A slight variation on the story Sally Speckle and Helen Rochester had been told by Ms Matterson, but it went to verify that Elizabeth Brooks had kept her secret about what had actually happened until she told her old friend before dying.

'During one particularly bad psychotic episode — he has frequent lesser attacks, of course — Aiden became convinced that Evelyn was trying to kill him and that he would have to kill her first. So he attacked a neighbour, apparently believing that she was Evelyn. And the reason for all of this was that because as a child Aiden had tormented his sister by calling her Cecily, Evelyn's second name which she hated, and which Aiden would taunt her with. He'd work Evelyn into a fury, when she would promise that one day she would kill him.'

'Cecily? So the name Cecily has bad vibes for your nephew, then?'

'Upsets him terribly. But only when Aiden gets one of his darker moods.'

Had he had a dark mood and murdered *Cecily* Staunton?

'Was the name of the woman he attacked Cecily?'

'Haven't a clue. Harold would know.'

'This woman was a neighbour, you said. So

she lived on Connoston Road?'

'No. Cranwell Street. That's where Aiden went to live after Harold sold the house on Connoston Road, when he could no longer take living with Aiden. Bit of a step down, but at the time the upkeep of the Connoston Road house, before Harold inherited a substantial legacy from a spinster aunt of his wife Elizabeth, was prohibitve. And there was little hope that Aiden would even keep the place clean, except the garden, that is. There he'd potter around for hours on end. Harold said that even as a child, Aiden had wanted the garden to himself and would become very upset if he had to share it with anyone.'

The twisted motive for killing his sister? Johnson wondered.

'At first when the house was sold, Aiden took to watching it, and used to wander back and sit in the garden when the new owner was away, which was reasonably often. However, one day he came back unexpectedly, found Aiden and called the police. It was around that time that Aiden got steadily worse and ended up in The Cedars for the first time.'

'You don't know the number of the Cranwell Street house, I suppose?'

'The woman he assaulted or Aiden's?'

'Both, actually.'

'Aiden is number 12. The woman lives three doors away. So she'd be number 9 or 15, depending on which way the numbers run. But you won't find Aiden there.'

'Why not?'

'He's gone walkabout. He often does. Could be missing for a couple of days or a couple of weeks. Could be anywhere. Likely to turn up in the park to bother his father. I worry that one day, he will harm Harold.'

'Was your nephew charged with assault after attacking his neighbour?'

'No. Not for the first time, Harold prevailed upon the woman not to press charges. I believe several thousand pounds changed hands.'

'Is Mr Harold Brooks at home?'

'Harold? I thought it was Aiden you were looking for?'

'We got somewhat sidetracked, I'm afraid, Miss Brooks. It's Harold Brooks I actually came to talk to.'

'Oh. Well, Harold isn't here right now. Why do you want to talk to him?'

Johnson sidestepped the question by asking a question, 'Then can you tell me where I might find him?'

'He hasn't murdered anyone, has he?' Though Charlotte Brooks's comment was flippant, Charlie Johnson was still taken aback by it. 'Harold's in the park.' She pointed over her shoulder. 'Just behind the house. Goes there every day.'

'Will he be long?'

'Hard to say. But he's always in the same place, facing the pond. He's not very well.' Plainly, Charlotte Brooks thought she had been given a burden of care which she would not have welcomed or, probably, with her hands found it difficult to cope with. 'Terminal cancer. Not long to go, I'm afraid.'

'I'm sorry.'

'No need to be. Harold is looking forward to the end.' She laughed derisively. 'He has this ridiculous notion that he'll be reunited with Elizabeth, his wife, in some beautiful garden where they'll live on in eternal happiness.'

'Maybe he will be,' Charlie Johnson said.

Charlotte Brooks looked at him with pity. 'Do you have one of those little cards you people have? Harold can contact you if he's of a mind to.'

'In the park, you said. Perhaps I'll — '

'Please yourself,' Charlotte Brooks intoned indifferently.

'Opposite the pond, you said?'

'Yes. If you go along to the end of the road, you'll find a laneway that leads into the park.'

'Thanks. You've been most helpful.'

As he walked away, Charlie Johnson was

chuffed. From a very unpromising start, he had learned a great deal, for example that the name Cecily had a very dramatic effect on Aiden Brooks. The murdered woman's name was Cecily. Might that have been the trigger for violence if Aiden Brooks had a pychotic episode?

Charlie Johnson was leaving when he turned and asked, 'Have we met before?'

'No.'

'I just had this feeling that we had.'

'Do you read childrens' books?'

'I have a nephew I buy books for. He's only four.'

'Then you may have seen me on a book cover.'

'You're a writer?'

'An illustrator. In some titles the publisher had kindly included my photograph as the illustrator alongside the author's.'

'Mystery solved.'

Walking away, Charlie Johnson could only think that with arthritis in her hands, Charlotte Brooks' career as an illustrator would not have long to run, if in fact it had not already ended. Maybe, and understandably, such was the reason for her discontentment.

* * *

'What's knocked you for six?' Helen Rochester enquired of Sally Speckle when she broke the phone connection with WPC Anne Fenning.

Troubled, Speckle explained, 'Anne Fenning says that she recognized the picture of Ruby Cox we printed from the CCTV footage from the station reception area.'

'That's good, isn't it?'

'Yes and no. Because Anne saw Ruby Cox in Jerry Cranton's company.'

'It might not mean anything.'

'Maybe not,' Speckle said uncomfortably. 'But it means that I'll have to question Jerry Cranton.' The DI frowned thoughtfully. 'Odd, that.'

'What is?'

'When I came out of Shadows earlier, I saw Margaret Cranton.'

'So?' Rochester prompted.

'Well, I've just remembered that according to Jerry, she's supposed to be in Manchester visiting her sister.'

'So she came home.'

'I suppose,' Speckle said doubtfully. Then, setting aside her thoughts: 'You take Sue Blake or Brian Scuttle and check out suite 306 in the Oasis Hotel in Brigham.'

'What will we be looking for?'

'Who, rather than what. A man by the name of Rupert Fox.' Sally Speckle filled in her Acting DS on what she had learned in

Shadows. 'Mr Fox buys a lot of expensive clothes for women. I think he's a pimp. The kind who caters for the moneyed classes, but nevertheless a pimp. Cecily Staunton alias Diane Shaft and Ruby Cox appear to have been on the game, Helen.

'And while you're doing that, I'll have a word with Jerry Cranton,' she ended glumly.

⋆ ⋆ ⋆

The lane leading to the park was longer than Charlie Johnson had expected, because it meandered before emerging on to what was now grandiosely called a paddock, meaning the council's budget had run out and the place had become overgrown. He made his way through briars and brambles to a meandering gravelled path with many offshoots that invited the more adventurous visitor to Southgate Park to explore. Many of the paths he passed on his way to the pond were mossy, which showed that Loston's strollers were either a lazy bunch or were not of a curious nature. But then perhaps they were neither; the deterrent to adventure probably lay in the paths' mossiness which, if trod, might end in one being carted off in an ambulance with a fractured hip.

On reaching the semicircle of trees facing

the pond, Johnson saw a man seated, his head on his chest as if dozing. The cut grass, under foot was slippery.

'Mr Brooks?' Johnson enquired, as he approached the seated man from behind.

The seated figure did not answer, and when Charlie Johnson reached him the reason for his silence became evident. Harold Brooks' throat had been slashed from ear to ear.

7

When she checked, Sally Speckle was told that Sergeant Jerry Cranton had gone home early, ill. And when he opened the front door to Sally Speckle, his drawn look suggested that he might not have been skiving off as she had uncharitably thought.

'Sally,' he said, not in an unfriendly manner but not in a welcoming way either. 'What're you doing here?'

'When I checked in, Grace Tompkins told me that you had gone off ill.'

'Bloody hell!' He laughed but there was no humour in his laughter. 'Are they now sending DIs to take a copper's temperature?'

'Can I come in, Jerry?'

'Margaret's away in Manchester,' he said.

'Is that a no?'

'No. What I meant was that there's no woman here to talk to.'

'Maybe that's best.'

'What do you mean, Sally?'

'Ruby Cox.'

What little colour there was in Jerry Cranton's face drained away to leave behind a dirty grey hue like the sludge left behind on marshland at the turn of the tide.

'Better come in,' he said, stepping aside.

Jerry Cranton led the way to the small sitting room where he stood, his eyes avoiding Speckle's, his gaze cast downwards like an errant schoolboy in a headmaster's office. He did not invite Speckle to sit.

'Want to tell me about her, Jerry?'

'How did you — ?'

'Ruby Cox came into the nick about the woman who was found murdered near the river. The reception area CCTV gave us her picture. And Anne Fenning recognized Cox as a woman she had seen in your company.'

'Margaret found out, you know,' he said, bereft.

'Found what out?' Speckle prompted after a long silence, during which Jerry Cranton struggled with his thoughts and obviously his shame. He slumped into a chair, seeming smaller than he had been a moment ago and older, too. 'Where to begin?' he murmured.

'It's always best to begin at the start, Jerry,' Speckle said with the quiet sympathy she was feeling for an old friend and mentor.

'I'm not sure how I even got into it all, Inspector — '

Speckle smiled. 'Inspector?'

'You're a copper asking questions,' Jerry

Cranton said stiffly. 'Best that we stick to the formalities.'

'If that's what you want, Sergeant,' Speckle responded.

'Yes. I do.'

'OK. Well, Sergeant, you were saying that you didn't even know how you got into it all. What 'all' would that be?'

⋆ ⋆ ⋆

DC Charlie Johnson secured the crime scene as best he could (luckily a semicircle of trees formed a natural boundary on one side and half of another) and called in. 'The prime suspect is one Aiden Brooks.' The only description that Johnson could pass on was the description Charlotte Brooks had given him of her nephew: *A long string of misery*. 'The body is still warm, so he can't have got very far, unless he's the birdman of Loston. Probably still in the park. Get a scene of crime team here double quick.'

⋆ ⋆ ⋆

'It's a funny old world, isn't it,' Jerry Cranton mused. 'How suddenly it twists and you're off in a direction you never expected to go. As the Americans say, sometimes life is a bitch.'

'Life has its surprises, true enough,' Speckle agreed philosophically.

'One afternoon about six months ago a call came in about a disturbance in Connoston Road. Jack Mullins and I took the call. When we turned into Connoston Road, there was an elderly man tussling with a younger man — the older man was the owner of the house. He had come home unexpectedly from a trip abroad and found this other man, as Mr Samuels, the owner of the property would have it, *rearranging* the garden as if it was his to rearrange. As it turned out, the younger man was a bloke called Aiden Brooks, who used to live in the house before Samuels bought it.

'When he saw us, he took off like a man possessed. Jack Mullins gave chase while I rendered assistance to Samuels. The intruder had a good twenty years on Mullins, so it was like someone at the end of the field in a race trying to gain ground on the winner. Jack's attempt was a valiant one, but he was soon winded and had to give up.

'And that was the beginning of it. The twist in the road I've talked about, Inspector.'

* * *

DC Charlie Johnson stopped an elderly strolling couple. 'Police. Did you see a youngish man anywhere about? What you might describe as a long string of misery?'

The man looked beyond Johnson to the slumped figure of Harold Brooks. 'Mugging, was it? Young layabouts who won't work, but prey on vulnerable people. Conscription. A couple of years under the thumb of a good sergeant major, that would do wonders, I can tell you.'

The solution was in perfect keeping with his military bearing.

'Eating dust in foreign parts instead of injecting themselves with heroin here. Best way to sort that lot out! Lead useful lives when they come back.'

'But the problem is that they may not come back, dear,' the woman said.

The man laughed gruffly. 'Problem solved, eh.'

'Please,' Johnson pleaded. 'Did you see —?'

'There was that man near the gate when we came in, dear,' the woman said.

'Yes, officer. Shifty type. I said to Edith. That one's up to no good.'

'He was tall and thin.'

'Drugs waste them like that, you know,' the man told Johnson.

'Which gate?' Johnson pressed. 'There are two.'

'The east gate,' the woman said, pointing

over her shoulder.

'How long ago was this?'

'Five minutes,' she said.

The time was right.

'Thanks.' Johnson passed on the information.

'If you catch the bugger, kick his arse for me,' the man said.

* * *

'Samuels had not been inside his house,' Jerry Cranton continued with his explanation to Sally Speckle. 'So when Jack Mullins got back I went inside to check. Just in case there was more than one intruder. When I went upstairs, opening doors, I came across a darkroom. As you can imagine, my interest was immediate. It was state of the art, so I popped inside to check it out. Unprofessional, but I couldn't resist. Samuels came in behind me and went into a fury about me poking about. Jack Mullins calmed Samuels down by explaining to him my obsession with photography and we parted on friendly terms, Samuels thanking us for our quick response.

''What's he got in that place, anyway, that sent him into a tirade like that,' Jack Mullins speculated when we got outside. I wondered about that, too.

'A couple of weeks later, by which time I had completely forgotten about the incident, I got a phone call from Samuels. Said he wanted to see me, and would I drop by that evening. I was shaken, I can tell you, Inspector. My first thoughts were that Samuels had changed his mind about me nosing about in his darkroom, and that he was about to raise it again. In my panic, I didn't even think then that had that been his intention, he would not have phoned me but a superior.

'Anyway, I went round as he had asked me to. He cordially invited me in. There were two other men there, don't ask me their names, I never got them. After a drink, Samuels began to talk about photography and the kind of pictures I liked to take.

'That bit of chat went on for another ten minutes, before Samuels asked me if I'd like to photograph something different. When I asked him what 'different' was, he invited me to join himself and his friends in another room. This room was like a film set, like a Roman palace. Every conceivable piece of photographic equipment was in there. Samuels called it his playroom. I know I should have turned and walked right out of there, Inspector, but I was intrigued. I suppose hooked would be a better description, like a junkie.

'Samuels went to a wardrobe and took out four outfits for us to change into. It was, he said, to be a Roman evening. I went along, because at that stage I didn't know what else to do. Then when I changed, I can't explain what happened to me. All I know was that a strange, compulsive fascination took me over, and I didn't have the willpower to leave. Or I simply didn't want to leave. Samuels was dressed in a slavemaster's outfit. He went to a concealed door in a far wall and opened it. Two women came into the room dressed as Roman slaves.'

Sergeant Jerry Cranton's sigh was world-weary.

'That was the first time I set eyes on Diane Shaft and Ruby Cox, Inspector. God, how I wish I never had.'

* * *

A sudden and very dark thought came to DC Charlie Johnson. What if Aiden Brooks had decided that rather than flee the park, he would visit his auntie?

8

Security at the Oasis hotel was tighter than a miser's hold on a shilling. To gain entrance there were three security stages before one got even a sniff of the palatial foyer, by which time the microscopic examination of Helen Rochester and PC Brian Scuttle had worn her patience thin and Scuttle's even thinner still. A swarthy Arab, built like the proverbial tank, whom they had sight of during the stringent clearance procedures, met them in the foyer to offer an apology that was perfunctorily diplomatic and worthless.

'We have many very important guests,' he explained, when Rochester's attitude left him in no doubt as to what he could do with his fake apology. 'These days, terrorists and kidnappers are very able and extremely cunning, officer. It is not beyond their capabilities to masquerade as police officers. We learned as much in the turmoil of Lebanon.'

Helen Rochester wondered how far removed from terrorism the Lebanese was.

Niceties over, he asked blunty, 'Now what is it you want?'

‘We want to speak to the occupant of suite 306,’ Rochester said.

‘Why?’

‘That’s none of your bloody business, mate,’ Brian Scuttle said.

‘Is that so,’ the Arab said. He turned to a group of security officers behind him and ordered, ‘See them out.’

‘We’re not going anywhere until we do what we came to do,’ Scuttle barked.

‘I’ll remind you that we’re police officers,’ Rochester said, in a calmer manner.

Unfazed, as Rochester reckoned he would be, the Lebanese replied, ‘Officer, if I ask you to leave and you do not abide by my request, a lot of important people in Whitehall will be very upset that you did not comply.’

‘Screw Whitehall!’ Scuttle said, moving forward towards the lifts.

His progress was instantly impeded by three of the security officers.

‘Perhaps you would care to check with a senior officer,’ the Arab suggested to Rochester. ‘His or her counsel would be invaluable.’

Helen Rochester was equally unfazed. ‘We’re police officers investigating a murder. And you’re impeding that inquiry. I’ll take my chances on arresting you, if you persist in doing so.’

After a moment's consideration of Rochester, the Lebanese smiled charmingly. 'Suite 306 you said, wasn't it?'

'306,' Helen Rochester confirmed.

'That would be Mr Fox's suite.'

'Then we'll speak to Fox,' Scuttle said.

'That's not possible.'

'Why?' Rochester asked.

'Because we've never seen Mr Fox.'

'Never seen him?' Scuttle barked. 'What's your game?'

'Suite 306 is for Mr Fox's guests,' the Arab explained. 'How can I put this — ?'

'Honestly,' Rochester said.

The Arab smiled charmingly again, like a crocodile might before it bit your leg off, Rochester thought.

'Mr Fox's guests use the suite for — shall we say, for enjoyment.'

'And pleasure?' Rochester suggested.

'Are they not one and the same thing, officer?'

'One might say different strokes for different folks?' Rochester said.

'How very astute you are,' the Lebanese said.

'Are any of Mr Fox's guests presently in residence?'

'No.'

'Then we'd like to see suite 306,' Rochester repeated.

'Ah,' the Arab spread his hands in a gesture of exasperation. 'Without proper authorization that would not be possible.'

'We could come back with a search warrant,' Rochester said.

Knowing that he was on safe ground, because by the time they got back with a search warrant (even if they got a warrant because the Oasis, Rochester suspected, would unofficially have the same protection as an embassy) suite 306 would be pristine clean of any evidence of Mr Fox's business acivities.

The Arab remained expressionless, unintimidated by Helen Rochester's threat.

Time to change track.

'It is our belief that a woman who was found murdered near the river in Loston, the subject of our inquiry, was one of Mr Fox's . . . *guests*.'

'You believe?' The Arab intoned. 'I believe many things, officer. But could I prove them? And in police work faith has little if any value.'

Squaring up to the Lebanese, Acting DS Helen Rochester held the Arab's gaze, refusing to flinch. 'The question is, are you prepared to jeopardize the outcome of a murder inquiry and the fallout from such an action?'

'I might consider your behaviour intimidating,' he said. However, after a brief consideration of his position, the Arab's stance changed from determined resistance to that of gracious host. 'I shall escort you myself,' he told Rochester.

'You're most kind,' Rochester returned with equally false charm.

* * *

Jerry Cranton continued: 'I know I should have walked away, Inspector. But, frankly, I discovered a side of me that I never knew existed — the Jekyll side. Or is that Hyde? I always manage to mix them up. But you know what I mean.'

His sigh was as weary as a last breath of life after a long struggle to remain alive.

'That was about six months ago. Since then I've been back to the Samuels house and other locations several times.'

'Jerry — '

'That'll be Sergeant, Inspector,' Cranton reminded her. 'Like I said, best to keep all of this on an official footing.'

'*Sergeant*,' Sally Speckle emphasized. 'You told me that Margaret had gone to visit her sister in Manchester?'

'She has.'

'She hasn't.'

'What do you mean?'

'I saw Margaret here in Loston less than an hour ago.'

'Can't be. I spoke to her on the phone in the last fifteen or twenty minutes.'

'On a mobile, was it?'

'Yes.' Cranton frowned, and then groaned. 'A mobile. She could be anywhere.' His frown deepened. 'Wait a minute, I was talking to her sister last night. She told me that Margaret had gone out to dinner with an old school friend.'

'Why don't you ring her again,' Speckle suggested. 'Now.'

He checked his watch. 'She's probably not home. This would be about the time she'd be collecting Colin, her grandson, from school.'

'No harm in trying. You might catch her before she leaves for the school.'

'I can try.'

Jerry Cranton punched out his sister-in-law's number on his mobile and got an immediate answer. 'Beth, Jerry here. Yes, I know you're running out the door to collect Colin. If you'll just put Margaret on the phone, please. Not there — ?'

He put his hand over the phone.

'She says that Margaret is out shopping with the friend she went to dinner with last night.'

'May I?'

Cranton handed over the mobile.

'Mrs — ?'

'Croke,' Cranton said.

'Mrs Croke. My name is Sally Speckle. I'm a DI with Loston CID. I'll come straight to the point, shall I. Mrs Cranton is not with you at all, is she. Please, Mrs Croke. I've seen her here in Loston only a short time ago.

'I see.'

'What's she saying?' Cranton asked anxiously.

'Thank you, Mrs Croke. Oh, just something that's come up. Nothing to worry about. Thank you again.'

Nothing to worry about? How DI Sally Speckle wished that that were true.

* * *

Charlotte Brooks opened the front door to DC Charlie Johnson. She looked flustered — on edge. 'You again. Wasn't Harold where I said he'd be, then?'

'Is your nephew here, Miss Brooks?'

'Here? No.' Suddenly alarmed: 'What is it? What's happened?' Charlotte Brooks watched Johnson intently. 'Why would you think Aiden had come here?' Her alarm heightened. 'Why, didn't you find Harold in the park, Constable? You should have. Shortly after you left I saw him there from my bedroom window which overlooks the park. He was in his usual spot. Harold is quite fragile. I like to check on him.'

'I'm afraid I have rather bad news,' Johnson said. Breaking bad news was a part of the job that he had never become comfortable with. Probably most police officers never did. And there really was only one way to do it — straight out. 'Your brother is dead.'

Charlotte Brooks staggered back into the hall and Johnson had to be quick to catch her. He sat her on a chair in the hall and picked up one of her slip-on shoes which had come off, and handed it back to her. The shoe was damp with flecks of grass stuck to it and he rubbed his hands together to dry them.

'Dead?' she asked in a strangled whisper. 'Harold, dead? Heart attack? His heart has been under strain from the chemotherapy.'

'Not a heart attack, Miss Brooks.'

'Then — ?'

'Mr Brooks did not die of natural causes.'

It took a moment for the import of Charlie Johnson's statement to register with Charlotte Brooks, but when it did, her mind was going in only one direction.

'It was Aiden, wasn't it?'

'I'm afraid it's too early to place blame,

Miss Brooks,' Johnson said warily.

'Of course it was that bastard,' Charlotte Brooks barked, springing off the chair. 'How did he kill his father?'

Johnson hedged. 'Well — '

She grabbed a coat from the hallstand. 'I'll see for myself then.'

Charlie Johnson stepped in front of her. 'Where Mr Brooks has been killed is a crime scene, Miss Brooks, and off limits.'

'Then tell me how he was murdered!'

Faced with Hobson's choice, between having to forcibly restrain Charlotte Brooks and answering her question, he opted for the latter. 'Mr Brooks's throat was slashed.'

'God Almighty,' Charlotte Brooks gasped. 'I told Harold that his lunatic son should be locked up for good, only last week.'

'We must not be too hasty, Miss Brooks.'

'What do you mean, too hasty?'

'Well, your brother might have fallen foul of a mugger, for instance.'

'A mugger?' She scoffed. 'You don't believe for a second that he was mugged, do you?' DC Charlie Johnson remained impassive. 'I didn't think so. Look, I told you that Aiden often sought out his father in the park. I wouldn't let him inside the door. Gave me the creeps to even hear him on the phone.'

'Things between them were not good. They often argued. Aiden would get very angry. Harold told me that Aiden could become quite threatening; that when this happened he became very fearful that Aiden would harm him. Aiden could be quite unpredictable, Constable. And as I told you, if he wasn't taking his medication his mood could become extremely dark.'

'Dark enough to commit murder, would you say?'

Charlotte Brooks gave lengthy consideration to Charlie Johnson's question before answering it. 'Yes,' she said. 'And I think I know why. Harold told me that the next time he met Aiden he was going to take issue with him about squandering money on prostitutes. Harold has raised it a couple of times before and they always argued. Harold was very straight-laced. More Victorian in attitude than new century.

'These women were grandiosley called social escorts. But were nothing more than well-dressed whores.'

Charlie Johnson thought: Cecily Staunton was well dressed. And her link to Mr Fox suggested that she was also the latter.

'Did your nephew ever mention these women by name?'

'Harold never said.'

'Did you ever meet one of these social escorts?'

'No. But I believe one of them was more or less living with Aiden. There had even been mention of marriage, which pleased Harold. He thought that marriage might settle Aiden down. Would marriage to a whore settle anyone down?'

'Has Aiden Brooks ever displayed clairvoyant powers, Miss Brooks?'

'Psychic powers?' she laughed. 'He's been trying it on with the police, hasn't he?'

'Trying it on?' Johnson asked.

Charlotte Brooks' laughter increased.

'It's a hoary old chestnut that my nephew pulls out of the bag when he needs to be noticed, Constable. An old trick. When, as a child, things would go missing, Aiden would use his clairvoyant powers to lead his parents to where they could be found or, more rightly, to where the cunning little devil had hidden them. My nephew is an addictive attention seeker.'

Leading the police to Cecily Staunton's body would certainly have made Aiden Brooks the centre of attention.

'Always has been. Once he killed their cat, buried it, and then led them to its grave, using his clairvoyant powers, of course. Harold and Elizabeth would play along and praise his powers. Stupid indulgence. Encouragement to deviousness was the last thing Aiden needed. A good clip behind the ear, maybe. But not encouragement.'

'Do you know for a fact that Aiden Brooks killed the cat?'

'Well, no. But it's something I'm sure he was capable of. And if he didn't do it, then who did? Poor silly trusting Elizabeth thought that she had a son with a *gift*, as she called it. When all the time all she had was a thieving, conniving, reprehensible toad! Now, shouldn't you be off looking for my brother's killer, Constable Johnson?'

⋆ ⋆ ⋆

DI Sally Speckle's mind was working feverishly, but not wanting to believe the awful thoughts she was having.

'Sergeant, did Margaret know about your . . . hobby?'

'Yes.'

'For how long?'

'She found out a week ago.'

'How?'

'We had a plumber in, an airlock in the tank in the attic. Clumsy bastard lost his footing and put his foot through the bedroom ceiling.' He laughed sadly. 'Just on the very spot where I had the pictures hidden under the attic insulation.'

'Margaret was hoovering the bedroom at the time, and suddenly these pictures were fluttering down round her like confetti.'

'She confronted you?'

'Like an avenging angel.'

'And you told her everything?'

'Yes. Hadn't much choice really.'

'Did she ask you where you took the pictures?'

'She did.'

'You told her?'

'By then I wanted to make a clean sweep. In a way I was glad it was over. I hated sneaking round behind her back. I'm really not the double life type.'

'You told Margaret about Diane Shaft and Ruby Cox, then?'

'That wasn't their real names. Shaft. Cox. Get it?'

'I'm not sure I do.'

'They're names to titilate, aren't they. Shaft. Cox.'

'I see. Did you tell Margaret about Samuels?'

'Yes.'

'And?'

'She threatened to go round and punch his lights out.'

'And did she?'

'No. She stormed out of the house vowing to do so. But Samuels phoned me the next day to ask why I hadn't turned up the previous evening. If Margaret had been round, he would have said. He wouldn't have phoned, anyway.'

DI Sally Speckle's thoughtfulness had Jerry Cranton's trained policeman's mind kicking in, and he asked fearfully, 'You're thinking that Margaret might have seen Diane Shaft coming or going at Samuels, and . . . and what? Well,' he demanded to know, crossly. And when Speckle hesitated to say what she was thinking: 'Did her a mischief? Is that what you're thinking? That's bloody daft, and you know it. Margaret is the gentlest of women.'

'Even gentle women, when scorned, can act out of character, Sergeant. Margaret must have been very hurt, and hurt can often turn to fury. You mentioned that Margaret had taken up a new hobby. A board onto which she glued newspaper cuttings to show that down the ages people haven't changed all that much? Can I see it?'

'Why?'

'If I could just see it, Sergeant.'

'Don't see why not.'

Jerry Cranton led the way out of the

sitting-room and along the narrow hall to a small room at the rear of the house. He switched on the light in a room made dark by a tree outside the window which cut off most of the natural light from the depressing room. The room was freezing, and she couldn't help shivering.

'No rad. Originally a storeroom,' Cranton said. 'Can't see the sense of Margaret locked away here this time of year, wrapped up in an anorak and scarf sticking pieces of newspaper on a sheet of plywood.'

Going forward, Speckle bumped against a small rickety table, knocking it over. An anorak draped across it fell to the floor, and when Speckle picked it up several balled up newspaper cuttings fell from its pockets. 'Rejects,' Cranton explained. But Sally Speckle's interest was in what was mixed in with the cuttings — a half-used tube of glue. A mental image of Cecily Staunton, her mouth and nostrils clogged with glue sprang to mind.

The same glue?

'I'll have to bag this glue,' Speckle said.

Jerry Cranton ignored the DI's statement. 'Told her she should get out more instead of spending her time in here. Used to walk a lot, before this took her over.'

The DI cast her mind back to the crime

scene and the fragment of cardboard that was found there bearing a partial print of what was probably a runner.

'*Used to walk a lot before this took her over.*'

Jerry Cranton's words rang in Sally Speckle's ears, filling her with an awful foreboding. Conscious of the piece of cardboard found at the crime scene with a partial footprint on it, Speckle asked, 'Does Margaret own a pair of runners?'

'She does,' came the reply she did not want to hear.

'I'll have to bag those as well.'

'Came prepared, didn't you,' Cranton said bitterly.

'You're a police officer. You know how it is, Jerry.'

This time Cranton did not object to being called Jerry, as he had since the beginning of Speckle's visit — no, interview. There was a comradeship in the way Speckle had said his name that would have made it bolshie for him to object.

As he went back along the hall to an understairs nook to get Margaret Cranton's runners, Cranton had second thoughts about *comradeship*. And began to think more about *pity*.

When Jerry Cranton handed her the

runners, Speckle turned them up to check the soles, which were spotless. In fact, too clean by far. Had Margaret washed off any earth from the crime scene? Or perhaps, Jerry Cranton, being forensically aware had done so?

9

As she hung up the extension phone, WPC Sue Blake was not pleased with her lot. The call had come from Chief Superintendent Frank 'Sermon' Doyle requesting an update on the file about the theft of some very expensive cars.

'We're in the middle of a murder inquiry, sir,' she had gently reminded her superior.

'Which is one part only of the overall workload of CID, WPC Blake,' he had flung back.

'Yes, sir. Of course, sir,' she had responded, hating herself for losing the bottle that her initial response had promised.

'Look,' Doyle had grunted by way of placation (hah!), 'I know you lot are overloaded.' Blake had been tempted to suggest overtime as a means of reducing the workload, but she did not want to be responsible for Doyle's attack of apopolexy. 'But a friend of the Assistant Chief Constable, who is in turn a friend of one Alex Crick,' there was the slightest pause before Doyle said drily, 'with a 'C', Constable — '

'Sir.'

' — Has had his Jag nicked from right outside his front door. And, apparently, it's got up his nose that only a mere PC's been round to soothe his distress.'

'DC Rochester is inves — '

'You mean Acting DS Rochester, don't you?'

'Yes, sir.'

'Don't try and pass the buck, WPC Blake,' Doyle growled. 'Like a boomerang, it always comes back. Just get on with finding the gang who are nicking all these cars. Any leads?'

'I'm not up to speed on the file, sir,' Blake said, wincing.

'Then get up to speed! And let me know ASAP how we stand. OK?'

'Yes, sir.'

Hanging up, Blake phoned Helen Rochester and got the name of the PC who had gone round to Crick's house.

'Isn't PC Hanley's report on file?' Rochester asked.

'No.'

'Then find Hanley and let him have an earful, Sue.'

Ten minutes later, Tim Hanley was moaning about the report on Crick's interview being one of a dozen he was writing up. 'And you just can't sit round until the scribbling's done, can you?'

'I'm going round now. Just give me the gist,' Sue Blake said.

'You? You just can't nick my case!'

'Do you want to tell the Chief Super that?'

* * *

Helen Rochester and Brian Scuttle looked around the scarlet opulence of suite 306 at the Oasis Hotel and, both arriving at the same conclusion, Scuttle was the first to speak:

'High priced knocking shop, I'd say, Helen.'

'Is that what this is?' Rochester questioned the Lebanese head of security who had accompanied them.

He shrugged. 'What is this *knocking shop*?' Rochester glared at him. 'What our guests get up to in the privacy of their suites is their business and none of ours,' he said calmly.

'It's also police business if that activity is illegal,' Scuttle said, crossing to a table with a dusting of white powder on it. 'Cocaine, I reckon.' The Arab remained implacable. 'I think it might be worth getting forensics in to have a look, Sarge?' The head of security was less implacable. 'I reckon this whole place could do with a good going over. There could be a lot of complicity,' PC Scuttle fixed a mean eye on the Arab, 'in the furtherance of a crime here. Prostitution and cocaine. A nice combination to get up a judge's nose.'

He grinned at the head of security.

'If you'll pardon the pun.'

The Arab's implacability vanished.

'I'm sure there'll be no need for that,' he said. 'If we can assist the police in any way, then it's our duty to do so, of course.'

'So who's Mr Fox?' Rochester asked.

'I suspect that Fox might not be the gentleman's real name.'

'So who signs the cheque or flashes the credit card for all of this?'

'Mr Fox pays a year in advance always, through a Swiss bank account. It's not an unusual arrangement. Many of our guests prefer to remain anonymous.'

'I just bet they do,' Scuttle snorted. 'This whole place is a right old den of iniquity, I bet.'

'So you've never seen Fox?' Rochester enquired of the Arab.

'No.'

'Do a lot of women come here?'

'I wouldn't know.'

'You're head of security, and you wouldn't know?' Scuttle questioned. 'Pull the other one.'

'If the owner of a suite chooses to pass on

the security procedure for use of that suite, then there is no need for security to worry.'

'What if the owner doesn't want this person to have the security procedure after he'd given it?' Rochester asked.

'That is not a problem. We simply change the procedure and the guest then informs those he wants to know of the new procedure.'

'We'd like to view your CCTV footage.'

'I'm not sure that that is in order,' the Arab said.

'Then I'll get a search warrant and then take it,' Rochester said.

'Viewing of CCTV by the police might unduly worry our guests, though I can't imgaine why it should.'

'We're only interested in Fox. No one else,' Helen Rochester reassured the Lebanese.

'Perhaps if you'd wait while I make a phone call,' said the head of security, after a moment of consideration.

'By all means.'

He left the suite with a promise. 'Won't be long. In the meantime,' a man who was conservatively at least six feet six inches tall and built to match, entered the suite from the hall, 'our Mr Howard will keep you company.'

'Shit,' Scuttle cursed. 'That bloke's in

danger of being struck by a low-flying aircraft.'

Their Mr Howard took up a position just inside the door, a virtual giant of intimidation. The head of security had hardly left when he was back.

'I am reliably informed that with a little editing, we can provide you with a picture of Mr Fox,' he said.

'I never doubted but that you could,' Scuttle said.

'That will be satisfactory, then?' he enquired of Helen Rochester. 'My superiors would not wish to add to the heavy workload the police already have.' And assuming Rochester's agreement: 'Then,' he opened the door of suite 306, 'shall we? The editing is already in progress and should be completed by the time we reach the security control room.'

The security control room was where most of those establishments were, in or as close to the basement as did not matter, and was accessed by a narrow steel stairs. On a monitor there was a head and shoulders still of a middle-aged man, and Rochester had no doubt that the unseen Fox was very expensively dressed, based on the evidence of his upper body. The computer printer chattered and a picture of Fox appeared.

'We'd still like to know where we might find Fox in his lair,' Rochester said.

'We don't ask our guests for addresses, officer,' the head of security said. 'It would be a pure waste of time. Are we finished?'

'That's a matter for my DI to decide,' Rochester said.

* * *

There was sudden and terrible alarm in Jerry Cranton's eyes. 'Margaret wouldn't kill anyone, Sally.'

'Margaret was hurting, Jerry. She could have gone to Samuels' house — '

'But she didn't,' he pleaded. 'Like I said, Samuels would have said if she had been when he phoned me. You're barking up the wrong tree.'

'When I say *gone* to Samuels's house, I mean that she might have watched and waited. Diane Shaft, or Cecily Staunton as we now know her, choked to death, her air passages blocked with glue.' The DI held up the evidence bag containing the tube of glue from Margaret Cranton's workroom. 'You know this will have to go to the lab, Jerry.'

'You think Margaret murdered Diane Shaft because of a handful of dirty pictures?' Cranton said crossly.

'No, not because of the pictures. Because she felt betrayed. She had the murder weapon to hand. And she lied about going to her sister in Manchester, I think because she wanted to be absent from the house without having to explain her absence. Where might Margaret have gone to stay in Loston? Has she a friend she might have gone to?'

'Margaret has a wide circle of friends.'

'I was thinking more of an old friend with whom she could stay without fearing betrayal?'

'That would be Amy Allsop, I reckon,' Jerry Cranton said.

'Why her?'

'Amy had a husband who liked to hit her, and for very little reason, until a couple of months ago in a fury he got a heart attack and left her a widow. Margaret had taken her in for respite a couple of times.'

Jerry Cranton spoke softly.

'Always one for the lame dog, Margaret. Shall I phone and check?'

'No,' Sally Speckle said very definitely. 'I'll pop round.'

Jerry Cranton was a defeated man.

'I can't believe that Margaret would murder anyone, Sally,' he said, utterly bereft.

'Jerry,' Speckle said sympathetically, 'maybe Margaret has a simple explanation for all of this.'

'Yes,' he said with false cheerfulness. 'I'm sure she has.' He held Speckle's gaze. 'I'll resign, of course.'

'Resign? Why would you do that? All you did was take a couple of dirty pictures.'

'You know that it's much more than that, Sally. I've let myself and the side down. I have no other choice but to go.'

'Don't do anything hasty, Jerry,' Speckle counselled. 'Give yourself time to think things through, before you go off half-cocked.'

She smiled.

'You know, you're not the first or the last to dirty their own doorstep.'

Jerry Cranton laughed sadly. 'A copper with a heart. Whatever next.' Speckle was leaving when he said, 'You'll let me know. After you've talked to Margaret?'

'I will,' the DI promised.

⋆ ⋆ ⋆

As commanded by Frank 'Sermon' Doyle, WPC Sue Blake set about reading through Helen Rochester's file on the theft of luxury cars in Loston, its hinterland and neighbouring Brigham. Her mood was pitched somewhere between anger and frustration; anger at having been side-lined from the murder inquiry, and frustration because she hated coming to an inquiry when another officer had been handling it. It was a no-win situation. The investigation lacked one's own stamp, and were one to solve the case the initial investigating officer would be none too pleased, because it would reflect badly on him or her, in this case Helen Rochester who, if Speckle had chosen her as the replacement for Andy Lukeson would do her no end of good when the next vacant DS post was to be filled and that would make Rochester her superior. And, of course, she had her own ambitions and knew that progress through the ranks was not smoothed by upsetting senior colleagues, or for that matter potential senior colleagues.

The file consisted in the main of a list of reports on interviews from the victims and a couple from known car thieves and tearaways with a fondness for driving upmarket cars which they could not afford. But, overall, the file was lacking in any definite direction which she might follow. So where should she start? Despondently, Sue Blake thought that wherever she started it would pretty much be going through the motions by going over old and obviously infertile ground. So she might as well start with the last theft — the one which had prompted a friend of a friend of the Assistant Chief Constable to lean on the Chief Super.

One Alex Crick.

With a 'C'.

* * *

'Shit!' DC Charlie Johnson swore on his third attempt to phone his DI's mobile (since DC Helen Rochester's elevation to Acting DS, he now thought of the previously informal Sally Speckle as the now very formal DI Sally Speckle) and for the third time got her message minder.

Alec Balson had been and gone.

'Straight forward,' had been his verdict. 'Prelim report as soon as possible.'

SOCO were now going over the murder scene, but were not holding out much hope of finding anything conclusive. 'A public place. Always a bloody nightmare,' had been the team leader's observation. 'More contamination than a plague site.'

A detachment of PCs had begun questioning people in the park, but so far had nothing to report. Some people had seen Harold Brooks but had taken little notice, because he was something of a fixture in the park. And every squaddie in the area was on the lookout for Aiden Brooks.

'It's like the furniture in your own sitting-room, isn't it,' one elderly woman had told PC Eldridge. 'You get so used to it being there that you take no notice. It was like that with him (meaning Harold Brooks). Always here, just like the furniture in your sitting-room, if you know what I mean, young man.'

Not able to raise Speckle, Charlie Johnson reluctantly tried Helen Rochester's mobile. Yesterday he would have been speaking to an equal who had now become a superior, temporary though Rochester's promotion might be. There was a DS taking early retirement which would leave a vacancy coming up shortly. Maybe Rochester was being groomed to step into Harry Porter's shoes?

'Sarge, is the boss with you?'

'Sarge? What happened to good old Helen, Charlie?'

'Just recognizing rank,' Johnson said.

'Acting the prick, I'd say,' Rochester flung back, annoyed. 'And no, the boss has gone round to Jerry Cranton's house.'

'Cranton's? Why?'

'She thinks he's got some explaining to do — '

'What kind of explaining? You're not saying that Jerry Cranton is in some way involved in all of this, are you?'

'That's what the boss is trying to find out, Charlie.'

'She's wasting her time,' Johnson said smugly.

'Oh? And how would that be?'

'Because Aiden Brooks is our killer.'

'You sound very certain of that, Charlie.'

'I am. He's just slashed his father's throat from ear to ear.'

'Why?'

'Charlotte Brooks, Harold's sister and Aiden's aunt, has filled me in on Aiden Brooks. He's a paranoid schizophrenic who likes to be the centre of attention, and spins this yarn about being a clairvoyant to put himself in the spotlight. He's a nutter out of control.'

'So he murdered his father to be the centre of attention?' Rochester asked sceptically.

'In Harold Brooks' case, I think it was less complicated than that. Aiden Brooks and his father didn't get on. Charlotte Brooks feared for her brother. And with good cause, it seems. Harold Brooks was a man of routine. He went to sit in the park behind the Brooks house every day. Even sat in the same spot every day. Aiden often met his father in the park. Harold Brooks argued with him about squandering money on prostitutes. Or, as Aiden Brooks would have it, *social escorts*.

Harold Brooks was of the old school, described by his sister as being more Victorian than new century.

'When Aiden Brooks chooses not to take his medication, he becomes unpredictable and has to be locked away in The Cedars until he's well enough to cope again. And he imagines that his dead sister, the one he probably topped, is trying to kill him. He attacked a neighbour because he got it into his head that she was Cecily Brooks come back to take her revenge on him.'

'Evelyn, you mean?'

'No. Cecily. Evelyn Brooks's second name was Cecily. She hated the name and she hated being called Cecily. But Aiden would taunt her by calling her Cecily. So I think that the name Cecily is some kind of trigger that drives him off the deep end when he has a psychotic episode.'

'So, what's the theory, Charlie? That Aiden Brooks murdered his father in a rage after arguing with him? And he murdered Cecily Staunton during a psychotic episode and thought that she was Cecily his dead sister. That sounds a bit whacky, Charlie.'

'Aiden Brooks is whacky. And there's more. Charlotte Brooks — '

'A very talkative type, isn't she? Coppers usually bring on deafness, dumbness and profound amnesia.'

'Yeah,' Charlie Johnson said thoughtfully. 'I suppose she is. Anyway, she says that Aiden's so-called clairvoyant powers were his way of putting himself in the limelight. Something would go missing, and Aiden would use his clairvoyant powers to find it, having, Charlotte Brooks believes, taken it and hidden it in the first place. His parents encouraged him in this nonsense. Elizabeth Brooks, Aiden's mother thought her son had a *gift*.

'The family cat was killed and buried and, hey presto, Aiden Brooks the clairvoyant knew where it had been buried, and Aiden was once more the centre of attention.

'Maybe this time, it wasn't a cat he killed. Maybe this time it was Cecily Staunton.'

'And to make himself the centre of attention, he called on his clairvoyant powers to pinpoint where she could be found?'

'You don't sound convinced,' Johnson said stiffly.

'I'm not sure I am,' she stated honestly. 'It's a big leap from a child seeking attention, which is not all that unusual, to Brooks wanting to put himself in the spotlight in a murder he had committed, Charlie.'

'Maybe when Brooks goes off centre, he's that child seeking attention again,' Charlie Johnson opined.

'A bit Hitchcockian, I reckon.'

'Hitchcockian?'

'After Alfred Hitchcock . . . The movie director . . . *Psycho*.'

'Oh, that Hitchcock.'

'Let's see what we have, Charlie. Aiden Brooks might have met his father in the park and slashed his throat. And he might have murdered Cecily Staunton during a psychotic freak-out. But where's the real proof, yet.'

'It's stacked against Brooks, Sarge. Once we get him in and start to work on him, he'll go to pieces,' DC Charlie Johnson said confidently.

'I'll alert Sally to Harold Brooks' murder. Why don't you run all of this by her when she arrives.'

'Thanks a bunch!'

After he had broken the connection, for some reason that escaped him (but he was sure that it was nothing Helen Rochester had said) DC Charlie Johnson's certainty that Aiden Brooks was the killer in both murders slipped a little.

Why was that? he wondered.

10

WPC Anne Fenning, out of sorts with the computer glitch that kept breaking up the screen and making it necessary to repeat everything several times to join up the snatches from the data base, flashed a disgruntled look at the ringing phone on her desk, demanding her attention.

'Yes?' Fenning said, grabbing the phone.

'Are you in charge of the murder investigation of the woman found dead on the river?'

'No. That would be DI Speckle.'

'Oh.'

'But I am one of the investigating officers, WPC Fenning.'

'Only a WPC?'

Fenning ground her teeth. 'Maybe I can help.'

'I'd rather speak to your superior.'

'Well, why don't you give me some details and I'll get DI Speckle to contact you as soon as possible.'

'I suppose,' the man said, obviously still not pleased to have to deal with an underling.

'And your name is?'

'Phillip Sullivan. But you might know me

better as Jack Upchurch?'

'Ah . . . '

'The author,' he said. Fenning could imagine her caller puffing out his chest.

'Well — '

'Never mind!' he said petulantly.

'I don't have time to read much,' Fenning said, wincing because she could sense that Sullivan or Upchurch was on the brink of ringing off. 'So shall I put you down as Jack Upchurch, then?' she said, hoping to placate the ruffled author's ego.

When he spoke again, he had lost some of his petulance. But she would have to tread carefully. If he rang off, her head would be on the block.

'Well, I suppose Sullivan is my actual name — '

'Tell you what,' Anne Fenning said, in her best diplomatic tone of voice, 'why don't I put your name down as Phillip Sullivan, and put Jack Upchurch, author, in brackets?'

Anne Fenning was relieved when he readily agreed and lost the last of his petulance.

'Now, Mr Sullivan, you're ringing in connection with the woman who was found murdered near the river, right?'

'Yes. When I was out running I saw flashes, like camera flashes, where this woman's body was found. I like to run late at night.'

'Did you investigate, sir?'

'Don't be daft. I could have been interrupting some strange ritual, might I not.' Fenning recalled an article in the *Loston Echo* some weeks before about a supposed group of Satanists who gathered along the river at night. 'Had I poked my nose in I might very well have ended up the second body, and that would never do.'

How could the world possibly go on without Jack Upchurch, author, Fenning thought.

'You didn't see anyone?'

'No.'

'Or hear anyone or anything?'

'No. Look, why don't I leave you my address and phone number for your superior to contact me.'

That put you back in your box, Fenning.

He reeled off his phone number, and added, 'Honeysuckle Cottage, Lambert Lane. I'll be leaving for New York the day after tomorrow to promote my new book — Honeysuckle in Crete.'

The phone went dead.

* * *

'Mrs Allsop?'

'Yes, Inspec — ' Amy Allsop's hand shot to her mouth.

Clearly, Jerry Cranton had phoned ahead. Not unexpected. But what had been the purpose of his phone call? Had it been to simply alert Margaret Cranton to her impending visit? Or, more sinisterly, prepare or coach her for that visit?

'Knowing who I am, then you know why I'm here, Mr Allsop.'

'Margaret isn't here, Inspector.'

Sally Speckle put a measure of steel in her voice. 'It's important that I speak to Margaret Cranton, Mrs Allsop. I'm sure that you'd do nothing to impede a police investigation.'

Amy Allsop was all in a dither, and Sally Speckle had sympathy for her position, caught as she was between protecting a friend and lying to the police. It was not an unfamiliar situation. Divided loyalties were not uncommon during a police investigation.

'Sorry for bothering you,' Speckle said pleasantly, seeing no point in distressing the woman further. 'Goodbye, Mrs Allsop.'

Sally Speckle got into the Punto and drove away. But she parked between two other cars a little way along the street to watch the Allsop house. She powered on her mobile which she had powered off, not wanting any interruptions while she interviewed Jerry Cranton. She had several messages. Charlie

Johnson sounded frustrated and emphasized the urgency for her to call him. Johnson's tone of voice, which was normally friendly, had become very official, his conversation peppered with *ma'ams*. She would hate to lose Charlie Johnson, but she would have to plan for his departure, she reckoned.

Anne Fenning had left word about a man called Jack Upchurch who had been out jogging and had seen flashes from what he believed was a camera from where Cecily Staunton's body had been found, and news that uniform had so far drawn a blank in their search for Ruby Cox. There was a message from Helen Rochester to call her back immediately, which she did, and she listened despairingly to the news about Harold Brooks' murder and the gist of Charlie Johnson's interview with Charlotte Brooks.

She saw Margaret Cranton coming from the Allsop house. 'Margaret,' she called out, getting from the Punto. At her front door, Amy Allsop was wearing a pained expression, no doubt fearing official retribution for lying to the police.

'It's all right, Mrs Allsop,' Speckle considerately assured her. 'No harm done.'

Mrs Allsop closed her front door.

'I thought you'd have more important things to do than get involved in trying to sort out marital problems, Sally,' Margaret Cranton said. 'I'm leaving Jerry, you know. My stay with Amy is only temporary, while I look around for a flat. But at my age and with my meagre resources, one is not easy to come by.'

Though she was sympathetic, Sally Speckle avoided getting sidetracked by the Crantons' marriage problems. She had come in her capacity as a police officer first and a family friend second, and saw Margaret Cranton's attempt to raise her marital difficulties as a delaying tactic, possibly to gain time to concoct a plausible story. Mrs Allsop's blunder had revealed that Jerry Cranton had phoned ahead, but the journey from the Cranton house to the Allsop house was only a couple of streets and had been traffic free, and therefore had not given very much time for Margaret Cranton to prepare.

'Margaret, Mrs Allsop's gaff tells me that Jerry phoned ahead, so you know why I'm here. Now what about the woman found murdered near the river? The woman Jerry photographed.'

'What's that got to do with me?'

'Jerry said that you stormed out of the house to confront this woman. Did you?'

'No. Well, I did, but when I left the house I calmed down.'

'What happened, Margaret? Did you

perhaps watch and wait outside the Samuels house?'

Margaret Cranton slumped resignedly.

'She was easy to spot.' Her laughter was hollow. 'I did have a very good photograph of her, if somewhat — ' She searched for the word, and came up with *angular*. 'I followed her to a house on Cranwell Street, not sure about what I should do, if anything.'

'Cranwell Street?'

'Yes. A house owned by a man called Brooks — Aiden Brooks.'

'How do you know that?'

'There was one of those little white cards on the bell with Aiden Brooks printed on it.'

'Did you see this man Brooks?'

'Yes. He came to the door to let her in.'

'Can you describe him.'

'It was dark, and he didn't put the hall light on. But he was tall and thin. And she called him Aiden. For some reason, he called her Evelyn. And she said, rather annoyed, you've been calling me that for two days now. Why? My name is Cecily.'

''Cecily?' he said, seeming confused, and then — '

'And then?' Speckle prompted.

'Well . . . angry. The thing is that I knew the woman the second I saw her, Sally. I don't exercise as much as I used to. But when

I do, I go for a stroll along the river early in the morning, and I've seen her jogging regularly. I figured that it was a strict routine. So the next morning I waited off the path for her to come along with the childish intention to pounce out, maybe to tear a few hairs from her head or maybe give her a black eye. But I thought better of it and left.'

'Off the path, Margaret? Where off the path?'

Margaret Cranton looked troubled. 'It's weird, really weird, Sally. But it was just about where she was found murdered.'

'How can you be so sure?'

'I had this . . . *feeling*. So I went to see. The police officer standing guard marked the spot.'

DI Sally Speckle said quietly, 'Her killer blocked her air passages with glue, Margaret.'

Margaret Cranton fixed a steady gaze on Speckle. 'Are you accusing me of killing her, Sally?'

'I'm trying to get a clear picture in my mind, Margaret.'

'It seems to me that you already have a very clear picture in your mind, Inspector. Shall I tell you what you're thinking right now? You're thinking that I had motive and opportunity. And I also had access to the murder weapon, a tube of glue. Pretty damning, I must admit. But I am not a murderer, Sally,' she said with conviction.

There was another person who had access to the murder weapon — Jerry Cranton. It was right to hand in that small depressing back room. Might the real reason for Margaret Cranton leaving home be because her husband had told her he had killed Cecily Staunton? Or she suspected as much?

11

DS Andy Lukeson's boredom with how things were done in the NYPD had not diminished, and his restlessness to be back in Loston had become ever more acute. In fact, he felt like the proverbial fish out of water. In the last hour he taken two loo breaks with the intention of phoning Sally Speckle to check on the progress of the murder investigation but caught between the need to be involved and the risk of having Sally think that he thought she might not be capable of solving a case without him (and that he had no doubt she could do), had on both occasions made him hesitant to phone. And now he was thinking should he take another break and risk the ire of Chief Superintendent Glass from Brigham CID, the course organizer, an ire which he had already earned in spades. Strictly speaking, he should not even be at the course but, short on numbers due to a sudden and unexplainable bout of illness (not uncommon when the brass began organizing seminars and courses) Glass had prevailed upon Frank Doyle to fill the shortfall in numbers. Doyle had obliged, provided

Lukeson's attendance did not come out of Loston's budget.

'I've already promised Chief Superintendent Glass that you'll be there, Andy,' Doyle had said, when Lukeson had expressed a reluctance to attend. 'Never know. You might learn something new. And it's relatively quiet here at the moment.'

Lukeson almost wished that the woman found murdered near the river had been murdered a couple of days earlier.

'It might involve some overtime,' Lukeson had said, in a desperate last ditch ploy (knowing Doyle's eternal preoccupation with the cost of overtime) to avoid the NYPD.

Doyle's smile was oily. 'Glass is picking up the tab.'

To hell with Glass and the NYPD. Lukeson left the room, watched all the way by Glass, straining at his leash, and a furious NYPD captain who was quick to take Andy Lukeson's regular absences as a slur.

Lukeson thought: I sincerely hope that I'll never be arrested in New York.

* * *

WPC Sue Blake looked about at Alex Crick's very oppulent and extremely elegant drawing-room into which she had been shown to await

Crick's arrival which, when it came, presented her with a man who was very obviously not pleased to see her.

'Mr Crick,' Sue Blake said with emphasis on the 'C' to avoid any misunderstanding, although she thought on first impressions that a 'P' might be more in keeping with the man's demeanour. 'I'm here about the theft of your vehicle.'

'Have you lot found it?'

Had she glimpsed a fleeting concern that the Jaguar had been recovered? Blake wondered. Might Crick prefer to collect the insurance? The opulence he lived in would suggest that he was not short of a shilling. But —

'Afraid not yet, Mr Crick.'

'Then what's there to talk about?' he said sourly.

'We're presently reviewing the file and — '

Crick slammed his fist on a table. 'Bollocks!' He grimaced and massaged the side of his right hand where he was wearing a plaster dressing. It pleased Sue Blake that the obnoxious prat had hurt his injured hand.

'I'm sure that in time we'll find the car and the thieves,' Sue Blake said, taken aback by Crick's outburst, which was at odds with the image of elegant living. In fact, Alex Crick's reaction showed him to be, as her Aunt

Harriet would say, mutton dressed as lamb.

'Will that be before or after you've found Noah's bloody Ark,' Crick growled. 'OK,' he yanked open the room door. 'You've gone through the motions. You'll find your own way out.'

Goaded, WPC Sue Blake said resolutely, 'I haven't quite finished.'

'I have,' Crick flung back. 'Look, this is all very simple. I drove home from my club. I came into the house to get a package with which I was to return to my club to give to a business associate. When I went back outside the Jag was gone. A couple of minutes, that's all it took.'

'Did you see anyone hanging round outside as you drove in?'

'No.'

'Someone in a parked car, maybe?'

'No. But then I wasn't really looking. You people seem to be unable to get to grips with these thefts. Two of my friends have had their cars nicked also.'

Nicked.

Sue would have thought 'stolen' would have been more in keeping with the Lord of the Manor. 'Nicked' was definitely a lower down the ladder expression, which spiked her interest in Alex Crick's roots.

'I didn't see any mention of your friends

having had their cars stolen in the file, Mr Crick. Did you mention it?'

He shrugged. 'Can't recall. The next time you come calling, be sure to be driving my Jag. Goodbye.'

'Sir — '

Crick swung angrily around. 'What now?'

'Are your friends, who've had their cars stolen, members of the same club?'

'Yes. But what's that got to do with anything?'

WPC Sue Blake was not ready to get excited. But there might just be something in what she was thinking that would crack the case. She recalled a note which Helen Rochester had inserted in the file that read:

Crick to front of house. Engine switched off. Why didn't he hear the car start up?

Sue Blake made it her next question to Crick.

'The front of the house. Was I? I can't honestly recall.'

'You had to have known where you could put your hands on the package you came inside to get, seeing that it took only minutes to return to the car.'

'Does it really matter what part of the house I was in?' he blustered. 'The Jaguar was stolen, and that's pretty much that as far as I'm concerned!'

'But if you were to the front of the house, would you not have heard the car start up?'

Alex Crick was suddenly not as cocky as he had been.

'Curious that, don't you think, Mr Crick?' WPC Sue Blake intoned.

What was Mr Crick up to?

* * *

'Are you going to arrest me?' Margaret Cranton enquired of Sally Speckle.

'No, Margaret. I'm not going to arrest you.'

'You really can't think that I'm a murderer, Sally.'

'Shouldn't you talk to Jerry,' Speckle said, concerned for two good friends, but also avoiding answering Margaret Cranton's question; a question she could not honestly answer.

Margaret turned back into the Allsop house. 'I'll be right here if you want me.' A little way along the path, she paused. 'You know, it's a real shock when you suddenly learn that the person you thought you knew everything about is a person you don't know at all. Never had known.'

DI Sally Speckle wondered if Margaret

Cranton was telling her that instead of discovering that Jerry Cranton had secreted away a few dirty pictures, that she had found out that he was much more — a murderer.

She was glad when her mobile rang. And more pleased than she ever could have imagined to hear Andy Lukeson's voice.

12

Aiden Brooks looked genuinely bemused when a squad car cut his path a short distance from Southgate Park, and an officer got out to challenge him.

'Aiden Brooks?'

'Yes.'

'We'd like you to come with us, sir,' the officer said. The second officer got out of the car. 'Just one or two questions we'd like to ask you?'

'What about?'

'If you'll just accompany us, sir.'

The second officer, younger and fitter, was like a tiger waiting to pounce.

'I don't think I will go with you, officer,' Brooks said.

The PC tensed and moved closer to Brooks, while the second officer moved to the side of him. The officers had, with smooth efficiency, backed him up against a wall.

'I'm afraid I must insist that you come with us, Mr Brooks,' the officer said.

A second squad car arrived.

'A bit heavy-handed for just a few questions, isn't it,' Brooks said. 'What am I supposed to have done?'

* * *

'Good to hear you, Andy.'

Sally Speckle's enthusiastic greeting made him happy that he had phoned. 'How's your murder coming along?'

'I'm not sure. Too many suspects. Including Jerry and Margaret Cranton.'

Lukeson's surpise lost none of its potency over the airwaves. 'You can't be serious!'

'I'm afraid I am, Andy.'

She went on to bring Lukeson fully up to speed on progress, or the lack of it.

'Jerry's got himself into a right old mess, hasn't he,' Andy Lukeson commented. 'And this clairvoyant rigmarole. What do you make of that?'

'I'm not sure, Andy. Aiden Brooks is a paronoid schizophrenic, and right now he's suspected of slashing his father's throat.'

'Sounds like you've got a right old mess on your hands, Sally,' he said sympathetically, but stopped short of suggesting that he should return.

'Brooks also knew the murdered woman, Cecily Staunton. She was what is fancifully called a social escort, a euphemism for a high-class prostitute, whose pimp, the mysterious Mr Fox, runs his business from a swanky suite in the Oasis Hotel in Brigham.

She's one of the women Jerry Cranton had fun and games with.'

'On a copper's pay?'

'No. Jerry answered a call to go to a house on Connoston Road owned now by a Mr Samuels, which was formerly the Brooks' home. Aiden Brooks was causing a disturbance there. Samuels travels a lot, and Brooks took to mucking around in the Samuels garden when he was away.

'Anyway, Jerry Cranton went inside the house to check if everything was OK and happened upon Samuels' darkroom. Jerry, being Mr Snap-it, couldn't resist poking around. Samuels caught him and was none too pleased, until Samuels realized their common link — photography.

'Some time later, Samuels phoned Jerry and asked him round to join him and a couple of friends for a photographic evening, which turned out to be a porn session.

'There's a suspicion that Aiden Brooks may have murdered his sister when they were children. His aunt, Charlotte Brooks, told Charlie Johnson that her nephew has always liked to be the centre of attention by using his so-called clairvoyant powers. I was thinking maybe he murdered Cecily Staunton and then reported her missing, pinpointing where she could be found to yet again be the centre of attention.'

'It's been known to happen, Sally.'

'Apparently Brooks also has a thing about the name Cecily. Aiden Brooks' sister's name was Evelyn, but her second name was Cecily, which she hated, and Brooks would taunt her by calling her Cecily. Then when they sold up and moved to a house in Cranwell Street — '

'A painful drop that, from Connoston Road to Cranwell Street,' Andy Lukeson commented.

' — Aiden Brooks got it into his head during a psychotic epsiode that his sister was trying to harm him, and he attacked a neighbour, thinking she was Evelyn Brooks.'

'So the theory is, that Cecily Staunton triggered a psychotic episode in Brooks during which he topped her because he thought it was his dead sister coming to take her revenge?'

'Daft when you say it like that, isn't it?'

Andy Lukeson's answer was diplomatically neutral. 'You never know with mental illness, do you.'

'And now we have a witness who, while out jogging late at night, small hours apparently, claims that he saw flashes like those from a camera at the place where Staunton was murdered, the assumption being that the killer was photographing Staunton's last moments, perhaps?'

'You're thinking Jerry Cranton?'

An unsettling thought came to Sally Speckle's mind. Jerry Cranton had said that he had taken photographs at Samuels' house and at *other locations*. Was one of those locations where Cecily Staunton's body was found?

'I don't want to, Andy,' Speckle said. 'But — ?'

'What was this witness doing jogging late at night? An odd time to be running.'

'When I was at Uni I used to often jog late at night. No traffic. No people. And it's quiet.'

'And bloody dangerous.'

'It used to help me sleep. Clear the mind after hitting the books for a couple of hours. Maybe it does the same thing for Phillip Sullivan aka Jack Upchurch — '

'Upchurch? The writer?'

'Yes. Though I can't say that I've ever heard of him.'

'You wouldn't have. He's not that kind of writer.'

'Oh? So what kind of a writer is he?'

'His publishers, if that's what anyone putting their imprint on this kind of muck can be called, would have you believe that he writes adventure stories.'

'I read adventure stories, Andy. I've got shelves of them.'

'Not the Honeysuckle Cocksure variety. She's Upchurch's heroine.'

'Honeysuckle Cocksure! Not a name quickly forgotten, is it.'

'Honeysuckle roams the trouble spots of the world, bringing baddies to book.'

'A formidable sort. Maybe we should let her loose on Frank Doyle.'

'But before she shoots, knives or blows her adversaries into a million pieces, she beds them and introduces them to delights that even these tough-as-nails blokes, and indeed women, never dreamed existed. The reason being that she's really not all that bad a sort and likes her victims to die deliriously happy and spent. Upchurch is a porn merchant. Of the really sick variety.'

Though it might not be the wisest thing to ask, Sally Speckle found herself unable to overcome her curioisty. 'You've read his books, Andy?'

'My information is gleaned from an American magazine article about Upchurch, Sally. Maybe it wouldn't do any harm to read some of his work in the interests of research, of course,' he said tongue-in-cheek. 'It might help you to get the flavour of the man's mind before you talk to him.'

'It's an idea, I suppose.'

The victim had her air passages filled with glue. It might be the kind of thing Honeysuckle Cocksure would get up to. A bloke who writes the kind of sick stuff Upchurch pens, and jogs when only vampires are about, might just be weird enough to make the leap from penning to doing.'

'Not another suspect,' Speckle groaned.

'Be careful, Sally.'

'A DS who worries about his DI. How charming.'

Andy Lukeson's laughter bubbled out of the phone. 'Don't overdo it, ma'am. It's just that I don't want to have to get used to another DI.' In the background she could hear the creak of the loo door. 'Got to go.'

'Thanks for calling, Andy. I appreciate it.'

Her mobile rang the instant she broke the connection to Lukeson.

'Bloody hell,' DC Charlie Johnson exclaimed. 'At last!'

* * *

WPC Sue Blake walked across the thick carpet of Alex Crick's club as close to being on tip-toe as was possible. It was that kind of place. It had the reverential silence of a cathedral and the luxury of a palace. The liveried doorman had taken her car to park (a mere saloon, unwashed, and with a spot of rust under its right head-light) suspecting that somewhere about was a hidden camera, the film from which would end up on the kind of telly programme that showed people at their most foolish. It amused Blake to watch while the doorman circled the club carpark several times trying to find somewhere to park her car among the sleek top-of-the-range vehicles that would not make it look like a wart on an otherwise perfect face.

'Hope you won't be long,' the commissionaire had said bluntly on his return, having cast at least a half dozen worried glances behind him at Blake's car, nestling between a Bentley and a Mercedes. 'What's a copper doing in a gaff like this anyway?'

A copper. She had changed into civvies, thinking that the sight of a copper in uniform at the august gentlemen's club might cause concern among those gentlemen who had little to hide, and outright panic among those who were masquerading as gentlemen. So the doorman was very intuitive, or more likely, Blake thought, readily recognized the species.

Interesting, that.

'And you'd be?' Blake enquired.

'What do you want to know that for?'

'Being a copper, I have this thing about asking questions. So please humour me.'

'Alfred Higgins.'

'Alfred?' Blake snorted. 'Not Alf. Must be the posh, scented surroudings, eh, Alf.'

The elderly male receptionist looked up from his contemplation of the gleaming mahogony reception desk at Blake.

'May I be of assistance, madam?' he enquired politely, but with an underlying note of no nonsense should any nonsense be in the offing. If she gave a little thought to it she would, she reckoned, probably be able to come up with his regiment — a man steeped in the service of his betters.

'I'd like to speak to whoever is in charge.'

'That would be Mr Hargrove.'

'Mr Hargrove it is, then.'

'You'd need to have an appointment to see Mr Hargrove, madam.' He instantly reached for a desk diary. 'I could check with his Miss Charters and — ' His pen hovered over the diary.

'Police,' Sue Blake said.

'Pol — ' the receptionist choked, shock making him speechless.

'WPC Susan Blake, to be precise.'

'I can't ever recall a police presence at the club,' he said, finding his voice, but not handling his shock very well. 'I'm not sure what the procedure is, madam. I mean, officer,' he corrected with less reverence, now that her true status had been established and she was not the wife or mistress of one of the *gentlemen*, of which Alex Crick, based on her recent visit, was a particularly bad example.

'What seems to be the matter, Stanley?'

Sue Blake turned to face the man who had asked the question.

'It's the police, Mr Hargrove,' Stanley intoned. 'To see you, sir.'

Like Stanley, Hargrove too had a regimental stamp to him. But, of course, of the officer class who might have dipped into the regimental funds along the way and, a scandal having to be avoided at all costs for the regiment's sake, had been quietly dispatched but in a benevolent manner. An officer and a gentleman (even if he was not a gentleman) was never simply booted out. That was strictly for the ranks.

Hargrove, though not as shocked as Stanley had been to find a copper in the holy of holies, still suffered a degree of distress.

'What do you want?' he bluntly enquired of Blake.

'To begin with, a list of staff.'

'Staff?' Hargrove was much relieved. 'Not the members?'

'Depends,' Sue Blake said, her reply

bringing Hargrove's concerns back in a rush.

'Ah. If you'll come this way, Constable.' Sue Blake followed. 'What seems to be the trouble?'

'I'm not sure there is trouble.'

'I don't understand.'

'It's just a line of inquiry to be pursued, Mr Hargrove.'

At the end of a long hall, they turned into a dusty, cramped office that was strictly functional and was as removed from the plushness of the club as Earth is from Mars. He went directly to the computer on his desk and seconds later the printer sprang to life, and seconds after that he handed the staff list to Blake who gave a cursory glance over the list and then folded it neatly and put it in her pocket.

'Thank you, Mr Hargrove.'

'Is that it?' he asked, surprised.

'Yes.'

'You don't need to speak to any of the staff, then?'

'Not at this time.'

When Sue Blake left, Hargrove slumped in his chair, worry crowding in on him. It had only been a couple of hundred quid from petty cash to buy a gift for an obliging lady who had quickly lost her willing nature when she had found that Hargrove's appearance of wealth was not matched by a robust bank account. The gift of a brooch was by way of inducement to look on him at least once more with favour.

She had not.

He thought he had covered his tracks well. But had he? There *was* that visit from the auditors last month.

On leaving the club, Sue Blake decided to take a little fresh air in the garden to relieve a headache brought on by a fickle car heater that when on cold became Saharan and when on hot blew Artic. The grass was being trimmed. It was much too neat to say that it was being cut. She was at midpoint in the garden when the sprinklers came on, and she arrived back to her car with soaked shoes and, it seemed, most of the cut grass from the garden clinging to them.

As she drove away, in the rearview mirror, she saw Alf Higgins showing a keen interest in her. Just outside the club she pulled in when a thought struck her. She phoned in and asked Anne Fenning to check the file on the car thefts which she had left on her desk and to pass on the phone numbers of the people who had cars stolen. Numbers got, she began to phone round. Twenty minutes later, reviewing the answers to her questions, she had a list of posh hotels, clubs and country houses all of which, the car theft victims had told her, had commissionaires (like Alf Higgins) who parked their cars for them. Two of the victims could recall the names of the people who had parked their cars. She added these names to the list she had received from Hargrove.

'Now, that is interesting,' WPC Sue Blake murmured.

Arriving back at the station, she passed the list on to Anne Fenning to check with the database, with surprising results.

13

Aiden Brooks, completely unperturbed by the functional bleakness of interview room number three, looked at DC Charlie Johnson and DI Sally Speckle with an amused grin.

'Something amusing, Mr Brooks?' Speckle asked tersely.

'Oh, much more than amusing, Inspector,' Brooks said, his grin getting even wider. 'Hilarious might better describe this ridiculous situation.' His gaze on Speckle was unwavering. 'I didn't murder anyone. But I will admit to, from time to time, having a great urge to murder my father. But, as far as I'm aware an urge when resisted is to be praised for effort rather than punished for failure.'

'You were in Southgate Park when Harold Brooks had his throat slashed,' Charlie Johnson said.

'I don't deny that I was,' Brooks said matter-of-factly. 'And I also don't deny that I spoke to my father. I often do when we meet in the park.'

'And Diane Shaft?' Speckle asked.

Brooks reacted angrily. 'I don't know any Diane Shaft!'

'Cecily Staunton, then? You would have us believe that you knew where Cecily Staunton's body was through a clairvoyant power you claim you have, Mr Brooks.'

'*Do* have,' Brooks snapped.

'I believe that you have not the slightest smidgen of this power.'

'I am a clairvoyant,' he ranted.

'I also think that you knew where Cecily Staunton's body was because you left her there after you murdered her.'

Aiden Brooks laughed easily. 'Sorry to disappoint you plods. You haven't done your homework, have you. I wasn't, shall we say, on the loose when Cecily was murdered.'

Sally Speckle felt a yawning hole opening up to swallow her.

'I'd been a bad boy. Didn't take my pills. So I was over-nighting in The Cedars nut house being put to rights. Check it out. Talk to Dr Marlowe. Sorry.'

'Well, you were not in The Cedars this morning,' Johnson said aggressively. 'You were in the park cutting your father's throat.'

'No, I was not.'

'Interview suspended at 7.06 p.m.,' Speckle said.

'I take it that my client is free to leave, Inspector,' said Charles Easton, Brooks's solicitor.

‘Not until I check out his alibi,’ Speckle replied.

It was nothing more than a face-saving exercise.

‘My client would hardly choose as a false alibi something which could be so easily checked, Inspector.’

‘Your client remains in custody until I check,’ she said resolutely.

‘Oh, Inspector.’ Speckle turned in the open door to look at an infuriatingly smug Aiden Brooks. ‘Cecily was wearing studs. Little diamond things.’

Sally Speckle did not confirm or deny.

‘I know I shouldn’t boast, but just to display the clairvoyant powers you think I haven’t got, you’ll find the missing stud, right ear I believe, in a dark place.’

Brooks closed his eyes.

‘I get a sense of water.’ He sniffed the air. ‘Stagnant water this time, Inspector.’

⋆ ⋆ ⋆

Alfred Higgins looked uneasily at WPC Sue Blake, and he had good reason to. She waved the database printout of his ‘form’ in his face. ‘Who’s been a naughty boy, then, Alf. Care to tell me what you’ve been up to here, eh?’

‘Up to?’ he hedged, his mean eyes darting every which way.

‘Alf, now you’re not going to be idiot enough to go down for the lot, are you?’

‘I don’t know what you’re talkin’ about, Constable.’

‘Let’s start with Mr Crick’s Jag, shall we?’

‘I still don’t know what you’re talkin’ about,’ Higgins said.

‘And his two friends who had those nice BMWs nicked.’ She studied the printout. ‘With a litany like this the beak will stamp on you like a cockroach, Alf. Of course if you were to show that you were mending your ways by helping the police, who knows, the beak might reckon that you could become a useful member of society and consequently be of a kinder frame of mind. Nice little earner, wasn’t it. You parking those lovely machines and — ’

Higgins shoved Blake aside, tried to do a runner but gave up when two young, fit and burly PCs blocked his path.

‘Don’t even think about it, Alf,’ Sue Blake said. ‘You’ll just give yourself a heart attack.’ She squared up to Higgins. ‘So what’s it to be, Alfie? Cooperation or, what . . . ten years inside, if you’re lucky. It could be more. And you’re not a spring chicken any more, are you.’

Higgins remained momentarily defiant, but as he considered his long litany of previous form he began to think that ten years inside might be an over-exageration, but not by much. Sensing his readiness to cooperate, WPC Sue Blake coaxed:

'So how was it done, Alf?'

Higgins took a small silver square box with a tiny antennae from his pocket. 'When I'd park a likely car for nicking, I'd pop the bonnet and attach this little beauty,' he turned the box over to display a sticker, 'to the car's box of tricks. When the driver started the car it activated the gizmo inside and in seconds it knew everything there was to know about the car.' He grinned. 'That's the problem with computers and electronic knick-knacks, ain't it. Some smart-arse can always steal your secrets.'

'I'd give a certain party a bell when the car left, and this certain party would follow on and nick the car. You see, when the ignition was switched off, seconds later the gizmo immobilized the alarm and popped the doorlocks. Then the thief got in, plugged in another gizmo into the ciggie lighter and hey presto, the car started.'

He chuckled.

'Ain't the education inside real good these days? The bloke who made these gadgets learned all about electronics durin' a three-year stint for knockin' over a post office. He made one of these beauties to work on every model.'

'A talented man,' Blake said. 'I'm impressed, Alf.' And she truly was. 'But now I need the names of certain parties and particularly the name and whereabouts of the electronic wizard.'

'Ain't I given you enough?' Higgins complained.

'The beak will want the whole story, Alf. And with a happy ending, too.'

'Bloody hell!' Alf Higgins groaned. As the PCs led Higgins away, he said, 'Crick wasn't done by us. We was goin' to nick the Jag, all right, but our man didn't get a chance. Crick left here and drove straight to a disused quarry called Querles Quarry, and dumped a perfectly good Jag into it.'

Alf Higgins shook his head.

'Now why would Crick dump a perfectly good Jag into a quarry, eh?'

'That, Alf,' WPC Sue Blake said, 'is a very good question. And I hope Crick has an equally good answer to it when I ask him.'

A half an hour later, after Sue Blake had reported back to Sally Speckle, the DI's mind raced back to her interview with Aiden Brooks when he had stated that Cecily Staunton's missing stud would be found in a dark place. He had also mentioned stagnant water. She knew of Querles Quarry which had, at the end of its useful life, been flooded about ten years previously to create a lake which was then forgotten about. A ten-year-old disused, flooded quarry would have lots of stagnant water. And the inside of a car in such a place would be very dark indeed.

'Don't ask Crick yet, Sue. Let's have the car raised first from Querles Quarry, and have it forensically examined. Then, I suspect, Mr Crick may have a lot more to answer for.'

'Has Crick form?'

'No.'

'Curiouser and curiouser.'

DC Charlie Johnson came into the office. 'I talked to Dr Marlowe at The Cedars. Brooks' alibi for the Staunton murder checks out.'

'Let him go, then.'

'What about Harold Brooks' murder?'

'No forensics. No weapon. No witnesses.'

'But Brooks admits he was in the park when Harold Brooks was murdered.'

'Nothing unusual in that. Aiden Brooks often went to the park to meet his father; Charlotte Brooks has already said so and will verify that.'

'He's got to have done it,' Charlie Johnson complained.

'We can't prove he did, yet,' Speckle said

tetchily, annoyed by Johnson's insistence when he should and did know better.

'If Crick's jag is in Querles Quarry, what're we looking for, boss?'

'A diamond stud, Sue,' Speckle replied, her conviction that there was no such thing as clairvoyant powers not anything as certain as it had been. 'And get uniform to round up Higgins' accomplices before word gets out and they vanish.'

How many more bloody suspects for the murder of Cecily Staunton were there going to be? When the phone on her desk rang, there was at least one more. When she hung up, she told DC Charlie Johnson and WPC Sue Blake about the latest findings from forensics, and the name of yet another possible killer.

'Ed Loss?' Johnson said disbelievingly.

'The freelance photographer?' Sue Blake checked.

'Yes,' Speckle confirmed. 'The footprint found on the piece of cardboard is a match for the runners taken from Loss at the scene of the crime. When he breached the crime scene, I had forensics take his shoes, in case he was taking any trace evidence away from the crime scene on them.'

The news had brought relief to Speckle that forensics had ruled out Margaret

Cranton's runners as a match, and that minute samples of soil found on them did not match the soil where Cecily Staunton had been murdered.

'This case has more twists than a sliding snake,' Johnson proclaimed.

'But what use is it finding out that it's Loss's footprint on the cardboard?' Sue Blake speculated. 'He crashed the crime scene. So he could have accidentally stepped on the piece of cardboard. At least that will be his story. It could be the difference between a rap on the knuckles and a murder charge.'

'Loss could also have wanted to muck up the crime scene to cover his tracks, if he was the killer,' Sally Speckle said. 'He'd know very well not to encroach on a crime scene. And Jack Upchurch saw camera flashes from where Cecily Staunton was found murdered. Loss is a photographer. But the fly in the ointment is that the piece of carboard was found to the rear of the crime scene. Loss had only been on the near side.'

'Then how is his shoe print on this piece of card-board?' Johnson said.

'Let's ask him,' the DI said.

'Talking about shoes,' Sue Blake groaned. 'Will you just look at these.' The WPC proffered her shoes, grass stained with flecks of dried grass embedded in the patterned soles. 'Went for a walk in the garden of Crick's club. The grass was being cut and the sprinklers came on. Destroyed a good pair of shoes, if I can't get the staining out.'

'Is that all you've got to worry about?' DC Charlie Johnson groaned.

14

The morning was typically autumnal. A frosty mist drifted off the river along Lambert Lane and clung to Honeysuckle Cottage, giving it the appearance of a giant cobweb. An unidentified cry, not a bird, permeated the mist, eerily lit by a weak sun trying to do its best to dissipate the murkiness but failing miserably.

'Creepy,' was Helen Rochester's verdict, as a sudden breeze stirred nearby rushes on marshland verging the lane. 'It wouldn't be hard to imagine something slimy coming out of there.'

'The only slimy thing living round here is in that rather picturesque cottage,' Speckle said, her verdict based on the three Honeysuckle Cocksure novels she had skimmed through before going to sleep; a sleep from which she had woken in a lather of sweat when a scar-faced, acne-pocked man had leaped at her from out of thick vegetation on the Yucatan Peninsula, fully and improbably erect and ready for action, direct from the pages of *Cocksure and the Ape Creatures*.

'Mr Upchurch?' she enquired, not needing

to, having seen a picture of Upchurch on *Cocksure Helps America*, in which Honeysuckle Cocksure came to the rescue of the Americans by wiping out every terrorist in sight, ending by killing the last man standing in a ten-page chronicle of every known perversion and a few new ones to the music of massed miltary bands.

'It's only nine thirty,' he complained. 'The bloody middle of the night.'

'Oh, to be a purveyor of porn,' Helen Rochester murmured in an aside to Sally Speckle.

'Don't you people keep civilized hours?'

'I'm DI Speckle and this is — '

'Oh, come in or piss off!'

He walked away, scratching his head of shortish black hair going grey.

'What an obnoxious git,' Rochester fumed.

When they entered the cottage Upchurch had disappeared. The clink of a bottle on a drinking glass directed them to a room halfway along the hall which turned out to be Upchurch's study. He jiggled a tumbler half filled with whisky at them by way of invitation to join him.

'No thank you,' Speckle said.

'Never on duty, eh,' he mocked. 'Does that go for everything or just alcohol?'

Speckle and Rochester ignored the jibe.

'Sit, if you want.'

'We're fine standing,' Rochester said.

'Please yourself.' Upchurch raised his glass. 'Ladies.' He finished the whisky in one gulp and refilled, immediately making a sizeable inroad into the second whisky.

'About these camera flashes you saw on the river, Mr Upchurch — ?'

'Someone up to naughties, taking dirty pictures, I'd say, Inspector.'

'What time was this?'

'Somewhere around midnight. That's about as exact as I can be.'

'Did you see anyone?'

'Not a soul. Neither did I hear anything. And neither did I investigate. I've told the officer I spoke to all of this already.'

'Late at night to be jogging, wasn't it?' Rochester questioned.

'Night is my time. I jog for an hour. Then I come home and write. That's why 9.30 a.m. is the middle of the night.'

'Funny old time for someone to be taking photographs,' Rochester observed.

'Some people have odd tastes.'

You'd know about odd tastes right enough Rochester was tempted to say, and might have, had not Sally Speckle cast her a warning glance.

'Have you ever seen camera flashes before,

Mr Upchurch?' Speckle asked.

'No. But I'm sure the river and its environs are full of strange happenings late at night, Inspector Speckle. Great name. Mind if I use it in one of my novels?'

'I'd prefer if you didn't,' the DI said bluntly.

His greedy, lecherous eyes took in every inch of Sally Speckle. 'Something like, Hornbeam Speckle. How does that sound?'

'Did you ever see any of these strange happenings, Mr Upchurch?' Speckle asked.

'Nothing that would interest clean-living ladies like you.'

'Maybe we should be the judges of that,' Rochester said.

'You know,' he circled Helen Rochester, 'you could do with losing a few pounds, darling. I have this wonderful recipe — '

'Stuff it!' Rochester interjected hotly.

'Sensitive, isn't she,' he said to Speckle.

'I think that's about all for now,' Speckle said. 'We'll be in touch — '

'How wonderful.'

' — If we need to talk to you again.'

'Sure you don't want that recipe,' he called after Helen.

'May I?' Rochester asked Speckle when she was about to close the front door of the cottage.

‘I suppose you’re owed that much,’ Speckle said.

‘Too bloody right I am,’ Rochester said, pulling the front door shut with every ounce of energy she could muster. The sound of crockery breaking, probably the delicate china vase on the hall table, gave Rochester infinitely more pleasure that the delicious cream cake she was thinking of having at lunchtime.

‘What do you make of him?’ Speckle asked, as they walked along the narrow lane to where she had parked the Punto.

‘Know what I think?’ Rochester said. ‘I think Upchurch goes running late at night because he’s a Peeping Tom. I mean anyone running at that time of night is bound to be.’ DI Sally Speckle did not tell her colleague about her preference for running late at night when she had been at university. ‘So what now? Are we looking for a killer who likes doing late night photo shoots near rivers?’

Speckle’s thoughts turned again to Jerry Cranton. She would, she reminded herself, have to ask Cranton what he meant by *other locations* as soon as possible. ‘Who knows what we’re looking for at this stage, Helen,’ she said glumly.

‘Has Andy been in touch at all?’

Helen Rochester’s question was too casual.

Was she saying in a roundabout way that it was time for her to get Lukeson back on the job? God, when would people ever accept that she was a good copper in her own right?

'I'm sure he has his hands full dealing with the NYPD,' she responded lightly.

The next couple of minutes back to Speckle's car passed in silence.

* * *

'Did you bring back my runners?' Ed Loss challenged Charlie Johnson the second he let him into his flat. 'I'm getting quite unfit.'

'Are your runners that much of a concern to you?' Johnson asked.

'They're mine; isn't that enough to want them back?' Loss groused.

Johnson produced a photograph of Cecily Staunton. 'Do you know this woman?'

'Don't think so,' Loss said, but the slight hesitation in his reply was not lost on Charlie Johnson.

'Sure?'

'I come across a lot of women in my work,' Loss said evasively, leaving the door open to later admit to recognizing Cecily Staunton, should that be necessary.

'Stop the bullshit,' Johnson said. 'Where do you know her from?'

It had become necessary to admit to knowing Diane Shaft (as Loss knew her) more quickly than he had anticipated, and therefore he had had little time to concoct a story. He did not want to admit knowing Shaft because of the video he had made of her which went beyond explicit. It was simply work for a fee (a very fat fee, admittedly) to him. But he could not expect a copper to understand that.

'I think,' Loss scratched his head, sending a shower of dandruff down on his shoulders, 'I might have done some work with her.'

'What kind of work? Or do I need to ask. Maybe, as they say, a picture will speak more than a thousand words.'

'I'm not sure I have — '

'You're bull-shitting again, Loss. And I tire very easily of bullshit.'

Resigned, Loss went to a walk-in wardrobe and came back with a disc, one of many stacked inside the wardrobe, Johnson noted. He crossed to the DVD player and inserted the disc. Johnson picked up the remote from a coffee table, hit play, and within seconds Cecily Staunton appeared on screen in a performance which sickened even Johnson, who had spent three years in vice before moving to CID.

'I only pointed the camera,' Loss said, 'as

Fox wanted it pointed.'

'Fox?' Johnson latched on.

'Yeah. But I doubt very much if Fox is his name.' Ed Loss scoffed. 'He fancies himself as a director, does our Mr Fox.'

'Fancies, you said?' Johnson pointed out. 'Not fancied. Does that mean that you're currently following his *direction*?' Loss was seething with himself for the slip. 'When is Fox directing your next saga?'

'You must have taken me up wrong.' Loss bluffed.

'OK. Let's go.'

'Go?'

'I'm arresting you,' Johnson said.

'What for?' Loss whined.

'On suspicion of murder.'

'Murder?' Loss squawked.

'Murder,' Johnson confirmed.

'Bollocks!'

'You knew the victim. Your footprint was on a piece of cardboard found at the scene of the crime. A witness reported seeing camera flashes where the murdered woman's body was found. And you're a photographer, Loss.'

DC Charlie Johnson shook his head.

'There's a lot of meat on them bones, Ed. Now, about this Mr Fox — '

'Oh, fuck Fox. Why should I care. Tonight.'

'Where?'

'Those posh apartments over on Greys Quay, where the Blue Stocking club used to be. Where George 'Pearly' Stevens used to live before you had him tossed in jail, when he had his thugs lay into one of your lot who hadn't paid his dues. Served Stevens right, too. I've met some bad lots in my time, but he was the worst. How is PC Bennett now? Stevens gave him a right drubbing, didn't he? Back on the job yet, is he?'

'Not yet. Being beaten unconscious with a baseball bat takes time to recover from.'

'Yeah. Not the kind of thing a coupla paracetamol will cure, is it.'

'Just give me the number of the apartment Fox is doing the video in?'

'It's Pearly Stevens's place.'

'Why aren't I surprised. What time?'

'About seven.'

'We'll be along.'

'Look, Fox mustn't know that it was me who — '

'He won't.' Johnson shoved his face closer to Loss's. 'That is, of course, if we find what we'll expect to find when we come calling.'

'My lips are sealed.'

'Now, to the reason why I dropped by in the first place, and that is, how did your dirty great footprint come to be found on a piece of cardboard where Cecily Staunton was murdered?'

'Cecily Staunton?'

'You'll, of course, know her by her professional name of Diane Shaft.'

'She wasn't the pro I photographed. It was Ruby Cox, a friend of Diane's. Some pictures for an American magazine that specializes in women being photographed at night, tied up.' He shrugged. 'Takes all kinds. Diane was supposed to be with Cox, but she didn't turn up. Ruby said she'd be along later. Boyfriend trouble, she said. Some bloke she had shacked up with who hadn't all his marbles, Ruby said. So I went ahead with Cox on her own. Only Diane never showed. Must have come when Ruby and me had left. And was murdered then.'

'Who else knew you were doing a shoot?'

'No one. Except Diane, of course. She often doubled up with Ruby.'

'At the same location?'

'Mostly.'

'Did Fox know?'

'Him least of all. He's a mean-minded bastard. He'd have my ghoulies in a jam jar if he knew I had used his girls without his permission and paid the appropriate fee, which my bank balance wouldn't come near matching. Sometimes Fox's girls moonlight.

They have to. He provided everything and didn't skimp, because he operated in the upper end of the market. But he took ninety per cent of what they earned. If Diane came along later to join Ruby and me, she might have met some nutter.' Ed Loss's eyes flashed. 'Heh, maybe this boyfriend got stroppy and followed her?'

'What time was this?'

'Ruby and me finished up about a quarter to midnight.'

DC Charlie Johnson wondered about Jack Upchurch, the late night jogger. Might he have come across Cecily Staunton? Might he be the nutter who could have crossed paths with Cecily Staunton?

'You didn't see a jogger, did you?' the DC enquired of Loss.

'No.'

'And you saw no one else?'

'No one.'

'Where will I find Ruby Cox?'

'Search me.'

'You're saying you don't know where she lives?' Johnson snorted. 'Give over, Loss.'

'Vanished. Reckon Ruby took the big bird after stupidly going to the coppers when she couldn't contact Diane. Could be anywhere by now.'

'Why would she do that? Cox didn't

remain behind when you left, did she?'

'No. Why would she want to hang about in the dark?'

'To wait for Diane.'

'Why?'

'That's a really good question, Ed. Maybe to have something out with her.'

'They were friends.'

'Nothing as acrimonious as best friends falling out.'

'Come to think of it, Ruby and Diane had a coupla bouts of handbags recently over this bloke Diane was shacked up with. Ruby said that he was dangerous and that Diane should give him the heave-ho. Diane said that Ruby fancied him for herself. Told Ruby to get stuffed.'

'Might Ruby Cox have fancied Diane's bloke?'

'Who knows. Birds ain't creatures of logic, are they.'

'Did you see Cox home?'

'I tried. The shoot sent my hormones racing, but she wasn't having any of it. We went our separate ways at the end of the river path.'

'So Cox could have doubled back, then?'

'Could have. But if she topped Diane why would she go to the coppers to report her missing? Doesn't make sense.'

'Not much does in this case,' Johnson said.

* * *

'Stagnant water,' DI Sally Speckle said, as Alex Crick's Jaguar was lifted from the depths of Querles Quarry and dropped on to the back of a recovery vehicle to be taken for forensic examination.

'Do you think that Aiden Brooks has genuine clairvoyant powers?' DC Helen Rochester asked, mirroring Speckle's thoughts.

'If there's a stud found in that car, I could be converted.'

Rochester shook her head. 'Brooks has got to be up to his eyeballs in all of this, Sally.'

'You don't buy the clairvoyant bit then?'

Helen Rochester shrugged. 'If, as you say, there's a stud found in the Jag, like you, I might have second thoughts.'

Charlie Johnson phoned to report to Speckle on his interview with Ed Loss, and the possibility that Ruby Cox had done a runner because she topped Cecily Staunton.

'Not another suspect,' Sally Speckle groaned.

'How did it go with Jack Upchurch?' Johnson asked.

'Nothing much there,' was Speckle's opinion.

'I was thinking, maybe Upchurch came across Cecily Staunton and tried it on? And maybe it all went too far?'

'It's a thought. Why don't you go round to Upchurch and put it directly to him and see what happens?'

'Did you find anything in Querles Quarry?'

'Yes. We found Alex Crick's Jag.'

'Bloody hell! Maybe Brooks is a clairvoyant after all.'

'Maybe he is, Charlie.'

Getting into Speckle's Punto to follow the recovery vehichle, Acting DS Rochester said, 'If Brooks is for real, I'm going to be the first in line for him to ask in the beyond if there's anyone there who knows of a successful diet.'

* * *

Three men who were respraying a month-old Mercedes behind a garage within a garage reacted quickly when the raiding party burst in. Two made it out through the back door and into the arms of four PCs covering the rear of the premises. The third, older and less quick-footed, saw no sense in trying to make a break for it, and simply sat on the bonnet of the Merc to be tamely handcuffed.

'OK, then,' PC Brian Scuttle said to the handcuffed man, 'let's be hearing who you're working for?'

'Haven't a clue, mate,' was the man's reply. 'Every Thursday a courier on a motorbike drops by with our money.'

'This is Thursday,' Sue Blake said.

'A cop who can tell the days of the week,' the man sneered. 'What next?'

'What time does this courier arrive?' Scuttle quizzed.

The man shrugged. 'Never learned to tell time.'

'You'll have a lot of time to learn the clock while you're doing time,' Sue Blake said.

'Done time before, darlin'. Risk of the game, ain't it,' he concluded philosophically.

'Always about half three,' said one of the younger men who had been apprehended and escorted back into the garage. The older man glared angrily at him. 'The game's up, Harry. It's every man for himself now.'

His anger made the man called Harry react impulsively and unwisely.

'Fox'll have your balls for this, Lenny!'

'Who's Fox,' Lenny snorted.

'Who indeed?' Sue Blake said. 'Seems to have his fingers in every dirty pie in Loston, our Mr Fox. Alert Custody that they're going to be busy,' she told a rookie PC along for the experience. Then: 'We're going to have a long chat, Harry.'

'Harry?' He looked about him vaguely. 'Where am I?' He chuckled. 'It's me Alzheimer's, copper. Don't even know me own name.'

* * *

Sally Speckle read the lab report on the tube of glue she had taken from the Cranton house for matching with the glue which had been used to choke Cecily Staunton and it made depressing reading, because the glues were an exact match, a result that could not have been more damning for Margaret and Jerry Cranton. Of course, there was some comfort in the fact that the glue was a very common and very popular brand.

'Bad news?' Helen Rochester asked on entering Speckle's office and seeing her glum countenance.

'Possibly the worst, Helen,' Speckle said.

Speckle handed Rochester the lab report.

'Damning stuff,' was her conclusion. 'Are you bringing Jerry and Margaret in?'

'If I do, it'll be the end of Jerry as a copper, Helen.'

'Can you really take that into account?' Rochester questioned. 'Murder's been done.'

'You're right, of course,' Speckle conceded.

'Want me to — ?'

'Thanks. No. I'll do it.'

When she was leaving the office, Speckle's phone rang. She left it to Helen Rochester to answer. The DI was getting into the Punto with a heavy heart when Rochester caught her up. 'They've found a diamond stud wedged behind the back seat of Crick's Jag, and it has a fragment of skin attached.'

Helen Rochester gave a little shiver.

'This means that Aiden Brooks was right about the stud. Kind of creepy, isn't it?'

'It is,' Sally Speckle agreed. 'Provided Brooks did not know where it was by means other than clairvoyant powers.'

'There's something else. They also found a haircomb with a couple of black hairs going grey embedded in it. Now who do we know who has black hair going grey?'

'What would Jack Upchurch be doing in Crick's Jag?'

'Research?' Helen Rochester said, tongue-in-cheek. 'Of the rough kind, the kind that can go horribly wrong. The fly in the ointment is, if Upchurch killed Cecily Staunton, where would be the sense in making himself known to the police?'

'Let's turn the screw on Crick. Ask him why he dumped a very expensive car in a flooded quarry. Charlie Johnson can put the pressure on Upchurch at the same time.'

15

Whatever you're selling, I don't want it!'

The front door of Honeysuckle Cottage vas slamming shut in DC Charlie Johnson's ace when he forced it back. 'Police.' He lashed his warrant card. 'DC Charlie ohnson.'

'There's nothing I can add to what I've lready told you lot,' Upchurch complained. And I'm a very busy man.'

Johnson kept his hand against the cottage loor. 'Won't take long.' He didn't bother with he *sir*. He did not think Jack Upchurch was leserving of the courtesy or the respect. Having decided on shock tactics as a way to attle Upchurch and open a Pandora's box (if here was such to open) Johnson took a gamble (because the hairs found on a comb n Crick's car might not belong to Upchurch) and said with blunt directness, 'Like to tell ne about your connection with Alex Crick, would you, Mr Upchurch?'

'None. Whoever he is.'

Johnson believed that Upchurch's curt answer was an honest one. 'And a woman by the name of Cecily Staunton?'

'Never heard of her.'
'Diane Shaft, then?'
'No. Look, have you got nothing better to do than play silly buggers?'
Upchurch had answered his question with the rapidity and certainty of a man who had nothing to fear or hide. Johnson showed Jack Upchurch Cecily Staunton's photograph and deathbed pallor was the result. Getting a glimpse of the possible Pandora's box waiting to spring open, DC Johnson applied pressure. His eyes on Upchurch's black greying hair, he asked, 'Would you be willing to give a DNA sample, Mr Upchurch?'
'Why should I want to do that?' he questioned defensively.
'Purely for elimination purposes.'
'Crap! If you want a DNA sample, tell me exactly why you want it, or piss off.'
'We could — '
'Yes, you could,' Upchurch interjected hotly. 'But you and I would be old men by the time you lot got past the million objections my very expensive lawyers would come up with. So stop trying to turn the screw and out with it!'
'Very well. We found some hairs in a car we recovered which we'd like to match. Black hairs going grey.'
'There are a lot of men with black hair

oing grey, Constable.'

'True. But maybe not as many who've been n Alex Crick's Jaguar.'

'I've already told you. I don't know anyone alled Crick.'

Charlie Johnson had a thought, and played hunch. 'Sorry. Did I say Crick? Of course I neant Fox.' The lid of Pandora's box weaked. Encouraged, Johnson pressed, 'Does Mr Fox own a red Jaguar, Mr Upchurch?' The lid of Pandora's box tweaked a little nore. Johnson followed his instincts. 'The red ag that you and the murdered woman, who vas professionally known as Diane Shaft, had un and games in?'

Pandora's box sprang open.

'Cox. Ruby Cox. That's who Fox said she vas. Don't you get it? Shaft. Cox. Fox liked o give his women provocative names. It's bvious that he switches their names to suit he . . . client. I'm bisexual, so Fox must have hought for some strange reason that I'd prefer Cox to Shaft.' And in reply to Charlie Johnson's quizzically raised eyebrows: 'Well, t's one explanation, isn't it. We, ah, shared Ms Cox. Fox and I.'

'Got rough, did it?'

Upchurch was instantly uneasy.

'Well, when I was leaving Fox and Cox or Shaft, whatever — '

'For the record, the dead woman's name was actually Cecily Staunton.'

' — were having a right set to. Fox was upset about some man getting free what Fox reckoned he should be forking out for. She said that she was going to marry this man and what was hers was hers to give. Naturally enough, Fox didn't agree.'

'Got heated, did it?'

'It had the potential to become very heated, yes.'

'Maybe even heated enough for murder?'

'When I looked back, I saw Fox strike her.'

'Does Mr Fox make porn movies?'

'Yes.'

'You've . . . sampled, have you?'

'I do a lot of research, Constable.' Jack Upchurch's face lit with the glow of a light bulb. 'Wait a minute. When I was leaving, the woman called Fox, Alex. But he introduced himself to me as Rupert. Crick and Fox are the same man!'

'Thank you for your co-operation, Mr Upchurch.'

'Just a minute. The woman we're talking about. Was she the woman who was murdered on the river?'

'Yes.'

'The same night I reported seeing camera flashes?'

'That's right.'

'Bloody hell! Dropped myself in it a bit, didn't I.' He became thoughtful. 'Fox or Crick likes cameras? Likes to photograph the action, you might say.'

'Sounds like Fox alias Crick is a very nasty piece of goods, doesn't it,' DC Charlie Johnson concluded.

On leaving, Johnson immediately brought Speckle up to speed on his interview with Upchurch. 'It seems that Fox and Crick are one and the same person, ma'am.'

Ma'am.

Charlie Johnson was still in strict, formal mode. Not a good sign for retaining him on her team, Speckle thought.

'Good work, Charlie,' she complimented the DC.

DI Sally Speckle joined A/DS Helen Rochester, WPC Sue Blake and her uniformed colleagues entering the apartment block on Greys Quay. They quickly made their way to Stevens' apartment and, without further ado smashed through the apartment door to reveal the sick scene being filmed. Before Crick could react, two officers had him under restraint.

'What's the meaning of this?' Crick ranted. 'This is a private,' he searched for the word and came up with, '*function*.'

'DI Sally Speckle, Mr Crick. You're under arrest on suspicion for the murder of one Cecily Staunton, also known as Diane Shaft. And quite a bit more.'

Crick took on the look of a trapped animal — a very dangerous trapped animal.

'We've recovered your Jaguar from Querles Quarry, and forensics have found some very interesting trace evidence.' Speckle's gaze came to rest on the plaster dressing on Alex Crick alias Mr Fox's right hand. 'Cut yourself, have you Mr Fox? Nasty things, diamond studs.'

The wind went out of Crick's sails.

'OK, Cecily was in the Jag. She was giving freebies to a bloke called Brooks. She said that Brooks was not business, that they were getting married, and that I could go take a hike. It got kind of heated.'

He held up his injured hand.

'I belted her one round the ear. Got this for my trouble. But I didn't kill her. She got out of the car, and that was the last I saw of her. When I heard about the murder, I got a shiver down my spine, so I sent him round,' he pointed to Ed Loss. 'He's a freelance photo journalist,' he snorted derisively, 'so I reckoned that he'd be able to get close enough to find out if it was Cecily who'd been done in. But by the time he got there, your tent was in place, but he heard mention of the woman having an ankle bracelet — Cecily always wore one. I panicked. I knew that if you lot got your hands on the Jag, you'd find something to lead you to my door. So I took advantage of the car thefts, reported the Jag stolen and then dumped it in Querles Quarry.'

'Well, you could always pick up one for nothing, as you'd been doing, masterminding the car thefts to begin with.'

'Me? I don't know what you're talking about.'

'Don't bother, Crick,' Speckle said. 'We've just busted the ring. Your, shall we say, *employees* are already singing like the dawn chorus.'

'OK.' Crick's panic was palpable. 'I nicked some cars. Ran a few birds, and did a bit of porn. But I didn't murder anyone. I was letting Cecily walk to tie the knot with Brooks.'

'Were you in Southgate Park today?' Helen Rochester asked, uselessly she thought, because she could see no possible reason why Crick would have murdered Harold Brooks.

'Southgate Park? No. I'm not the outdoor type.'

'Good,' Sally Speckle said. 'It'll make your time inside all the more bearable.'

'I didn't murder anyone,' Crick protested as he was led away.

* * *

'Murder?' Frank 'Sermon' Doyle boomed. 'Crick,' his mind already racing ahead. 'A friend of a friend of the Chief Constable!'

'There's also car theft. Living off immoral earnings. Making sick porn videos. And wasting police time.'

'You're sure, Speckle? About the murder bit? The rest is small change compared to that.' And when Sally Speckle hesitated. 'What is it you're not sure about, Inspector? Tell me it's the murder, if it's got to be anything.'

'Crick alias Fox is a nasty piece of work — '

'But?'

'A murderer?' Speckle hunched her shoulders. 'I'm not so sure.'

'Have you formally charged Crick with murder?'

'Not yet.'

'Well, don't. Not until you're absolutely certain. Maybe another DI would bring fresh thinking to bear.'

Sally Speckle was stunned.

'You've got, at most, two days, Speckle,'

Doyle stated. 'After that you'll have to step aside.'

She should have been incensed, but instead Sally Speckle was gloomy. She was on her way back to her office when she stopped to look out a window, taking time out to regain her composure before reporting to the team. A heavy shower was in progress, the third in quick succession. A woman who had parked in front of the station was fumbling with an umbrella which refused to open. She threw the umbrella back into the car and ran to the station entrance, unwisely across the patch of recently cut grass that served as a garden of sorts, and immediately realized the damage the soggy patch had done to her shoes, from which she had to clean the grass cuttings and mud with a tissue which she carelessly discarded, flouting Loston's litter laws for which, now drenched and muddied, the woman would not have cared a fig about. 'Some days are like that,' Speckle said sympathetically, and walked on, but only for a short distance before coming up short.

She reckoned she knew who had murdered Harold Brooks and Cecily Staunton. And she would be certain of the killer's identity if DC Charlie Johnson's answer to her question was the one she hoped it would be.

16

'Was the grass in Southgate Park being cut, or had it been recently cut, when you went to find Harold Brooks, Charlie?' she enquired of Johnson.

'Near where Harold Brooks was, yes. Why?'

'Did the grass stick to your shoes, like it stuck to Sue Blake's, when she went walkabout at Crick's club?'

'Yeah.'

'Now, think very carefully, Charlie. When you returned to the Brooks house, had Charlotte Brooks' shoes wet grass on them?'

A light lit in Charlie Johnson's eyes. 'That's what was odd. But I just couldn't put my finger on it at the time. Charlotte Brooks' shoes were wet and had wet grass on them. And a whitish guck like — '

'Ashes?' Sally Speckle suggested.

'Could be, I suppose. I noticed, because she slipped out of her shoe and I picked it up and handed it back to her.' Johnson exclaimed as the pieces of the jigsaw fell into place. 'Charlotte Brooks murdered Harold Brooks. While I was taking the long way round, she went through the rotten fence at the end of her garden directly into Southgate Park, got to Harold Brooks before me, and murdered him.'

'Yes, I believe that's exactly how it happened, Charlie,' Speckle said.

'Bloody audacious, that,' Johnson said, with no small degree of admiration. 'Charlotte Brooks next stop, I reckon.'

'First, I must make a phone call. Charles Easton was Aiden Brooks' solicitor when we pulled him in for questioning. I'm hoping that Easton is also the Brooks' family solicitor.'

* * *

Approaching Charlotte Brooks' house half an hour later, Speckle had to swerve sharply to avoid a refuse truck, driven in the cavalier fashion such vehicles are often driven in. The road was a long one which gave Johnson (a typical passenger-seat driver) time to get his breath back before they reached the Brooks' house. Still a touch rattled, he knocked against the refuse bin outside the Brooks' house and nearly upended it.

'You again,' Charlotte Brooks said annoyedly, on seeing Charlie Johnson on her doorstep. Her eyes flashed to Sally Speckle. 'And with company. How thrilling.'

Sally introduced herself. 'May we come in?'
'Must you?'
'I think it would be best, Miss Brooks.'
Charlotte Brooks walked ahead. 'Shut the door after you.' She turned into a room further along the hall. Speckle and Johnson followed. 'If you sit down, don't lean back. It ruins the cushions.'
Speckle and Johnson remained standing. On a nearby table, Johnson's eye caught sight of a broken figurine on the sofa, a dancing lady with a missing arm.
'Cat again?' Johnson asked.
'No. Me this time. Dropped it when I was dusting. A dab of glue and it'll be as good as new.' She looked curiously from one to the other. 'So?'
'Miss Brooks,' Speckle said. 'It is our belief that you murdered your brother and a woman named Cecily Staunton.'
'She goes straight for the jugular, doesn't she,' Charlotte Brooks said to Johnson. 'Must be a bitch to work for.' Her gaze was steady on Speckle. 'Insane, as she is.'
'When DC Johnson returned to the house, after your brother had been murdered — '
'By his son.'
' — to check on your safety, you had wet grass on your shoes.'
'I had been in the garden.'

Charlotte Brooks was quick.

Speckle looked out the window to the overgrown garden, pleased on seeing a burned patch on it, and the rotten fence at the end of the garden. 'Wet, cut grass, Miss Brooks,' Speckle emphasized. 'A bit of a jungle out there, isn't it. Hasn't been cut in an age.' There was, Speckle thought, the briefest flicker of concern in Charlotte Brooks' eyes. 'The wet grass on your shoes, I put it to you, came from Southgate Park. In fact, from where your brother was sitting.'

'How very — ' Charlotte Brooks searched for a description of Speckle's as yet unproven theory, and came up with, 'far fetched. You should really be writing detective stories, Inspector.'

Speckle continued, 'When DC Johnson went to go to the park, the long way round, you left the house and reached the park through the fence at the end of your garden. You had the edge on him, because you knew exactly where to find your brother — sitting opposite the pond, where he always sat. You reached your brother before DC Johnson, cut your brother's throat, hid and waited for your chance to return to the house the same way as you left.'

'A very risky strategy, don't you think, Inspector,' said Charlotte Brooks. 'With police crawling all over the place.' Her eyes sparkled. 'But highly entertaining.' She was not unduly worried, and with good reason, Speckle thought. Because if Charlotte Brooks held her nerve, the chance of the Crown Prosecution Service bringing the case to court on largely unprovable evidence was very slim indeed. And the chance of her asking the CPS to do so was even slimmer still. But there was nothing for it but to press on.

'What murder is without risk, Miss Brooks?' Sally Speckle's gaze fixed on the black patch in the garden. 'Is that where you burned your blood-stained clothes?'

'Really,' Charlotte Brooks said. 'You really are becoming tedious, Inspector. If you can prove one shred of this, and you can't because you're talking through your hat, then arrest me. I often burn old clothes in the garden. It would never do to snarl up the refuse truck's mechanism. Look, my nephew murdered his father, it's as plain and simple as that. They've been at odds for years. I warned Harold not to be alone with Aiden. He's mentally unstable. In fact, I made my concerns known to DC Johnson. And what kind of a fool do you think I am? To commit murder with a police officer on my doorstep?'

'It is precisely because he was on your

loorstep that you took the opportunity to
nurder your brother, after first painting your
ıephew black, so that he would automatically
ɔe the prime suspect for his father's murder.'
'Oh, dear. You do paint me black, don't
'ou, Inspector.'
'You're a very clever woman, Miss Brooks.
t might even have worked, if you had burned
he wet shoes with the blood-stained
:lothing.' Speckle sighed. 'There's always that
ittle something, isn't there.'
'Why would I murder Harold?' Charlotte
3rooks laughed, but the slight tremor in her
aughter gave Sally Speckle a glimmer of
ıope. 'What possible motive would I have
ıad?'
'One of the oldest in the book,' Speckle
said. 'Financial gain, pure and simple. Or
should I say more properly, financial loss.
Harold Brooks was planning on changing his
will in favour of Aiden Brooks, delighted as
ıe was at the news of his impending marriage
:o Cecily Staunton, or perhaps you'd know
ıer better as Diane Shaft, the social escort
who was to be your nephew's new wife.'
'That's rubbish,' Charlotte Brooks dis-
missed curtly. 'Harold had no plans to change
ıis will.'
'I've spoken to Mr Easton, your brother's
solicitor, Miss Brooks. He's confirmed that

your brother had arranged with him to call to the house for the purpose of changing his will.'

'I knew nothing of this.' There was an edginess in Charlotte Brooks that had not been there before. She held out her hands. 'I have severe arthritis, in my knees and hips as well as in my hands. I have to rub in a special herbal prepartion several times a day to relieve the pain. You'd be laughed out of court if you attempted to tell a judge and jury that I did what you've described.'

'A jury might also think that there's no gain without pain, Ms Brooks.'

'Then arrest me, or clear off!' Brooks said defiantly.

The interview had reached a critical point.

Sensing the DI's dilemma, Charlotte Brooks said, 'You'll see yourself out, won't you, Inspector.'

Speckle was on the point of leaving when Charlie Johnson piped up, 'You were rubbing that gel into your hands when I left to go to the park. I'm counting that in your hurry, you didn't take the time to wash it off before you went on your errand of murder. That being the case, traces of it will be found on Harold Brooks's clothes. The lab will find the minutest trace of that gel,' Johnson said.

'So what,' said Brooks scoffingly. 'Harold

ved here. I looked after him. Of course your recious lab will find traces of the gel on him. ow, I am rather tired — '

DI Sally Speckle was about to withdraw to egroup when her gaze came to rest on the roken figurine on the table, and Charlotte Brooks words echoed in her head. '*A dab of lue and it will be as good as new*.' At the ame moment the sound of the refuse truck utside the house acted like a spark to petrol.

'The refuse truck, Charlie. Get the refuse in before they tip it!'

Johnson raced outside and grabbed the bin ack just as it was being loaded on to the fting gear. 'Police,' the DC said, as the man e had shoved aside to get at the bin gave him n ugly look.

Arriving on the scene, Speckle ordered, Empty it.'

Tipping the bin, Charlie Johnson said, 'I ope whatever you're looking for is in here.'

'If it isn't, we're back on the beat, Charlie.'

The pile of rubbish lay on the footpath like mortal sin on an otherwise unblemished oul. Speckle poked at it with her toe. When he saw Charlotte Brooks at the window vatching her intently, she knew without loubt that she was on the right track.

'Is this what you might be looking for?' ohnson said, using a handkerchief to retrieve a steak knife from the rubbish. He pointed to a crust of dried blood wedged in where the handle was attached to the knife.

'One of the items,' Speckle said. 'But I'm also hoping to find — ' She stooped down and picked up a used tube of glue with the tips of her fingers; the same brand of glue that Margaret Cranton used, so it would be a match with the glue that choked Cecily Staunton. She turned and held up the steak knife and the used tube of glue to Charlotte Brooks. The result was startling. Brooks resignation was complete. 'Leave the rubbish exactly where it is,' she ordered the refuse men.

'Never reckoned on doin' nothin' else,' one of the refuse men replied sourly.

'Lets go back inside, Charlie.'

Charlotte Brooks was sitting where she had been when they had rushed outside, calm and resigned.

'This glue you used to mend your ornaments with is the same glue you used to choke Cecily Staunton with, Miss Brook,' Speckle charged.

'Yes. I wanted her to suffer. She did. She was going to marry Aiden. Harold was pleased. Thought it would settle Aiden down. And the precious Brooks line would be continued. Then one day I was going hopping. I forgot my purse and turned back. Harold was in the study talking on the phone o Mr Easton, the family solicitor. Harold wanted him to come round because he wanted to change his will.'

Her face became bitter.

'Aiden and his new wife were to receive the ion's share of Harold's fortune, when previously I had been the sole beneficiary, other than a token sum to Aiden. My thanks or taking Harold in and caring for him.' She held out her hands again. 'I used to illustrate children's books. I needed Harold's money badly.'

Charlotte Brooks went to look out of the window.

'Yes, I murdered Harold, Inspector. Your recreation of what happened was uncanny. You might have been right there, watching. God, the pain of trying to run on half-crippled legs. But it was worth it. I had earned that money. So now that it was being stolen from me, there had to be retribution.' She turned from the window. 'After all, it's only fair. So I decided on the punishment. Harold would forfeit his life for his treachery. And Aiden would forfeit his whore. Perhaps at some time later, his life, too. I watched the house in Cranwell Street until I saw his whore. I didn't at that stage have a plan. But fate intervened. One night by chance, driving past, I saw her go along the river path. Purely on impulse, I followed her. She came to a spot where she called out to someone called Ruby Cox. Getting no response, she began to call to someone called Loss — Ed Loss, I think. But there was no one there, so I crept up behind her, picked up a rock, and hit her on the side of the head. She fell, stunned. I was ready to bash her skull in, when a tube of glue I had been using earlier fell out of my pocket and I had a most marvellous idea. For some reason, there was some rope lying around . . . '

One of Ed Loss's props, Speckle reckoned.

'I tied her up, and then filled her mouth and nose with the glue. It's the quick-setting variety. And I watched her choke to death. While she was dying I told her who I was, and why I had decided to kill her.' Charlotte Brooks smiled. 'I thought it rather decent that I took the time, Inspector. The civilized thing to do, wouldn't you say? However, I am pleased to say that I terrfied the whore out of her mind.'

Charlotte Brooks crossed the room to the door.

'Shall we go, Inspector?'

* * *

'You're turning into one bloody fine copper, Speckle,' 'Sermon' Doyle congratulated Sally. 'Two murders solved and a car theft ring bunched. And,' he added exuberantly, 'without overtime, too.'

'A team effort, sir,' Speckle said graciously.

'Now, this Johnson and Rochester business. Charlie Johnson's bunged in a request for a transfer, and I have to admit that I can see his point of view. Rochester's got less service.'

'Isn't it time that ability and suitability became the criteria for promotion, sir.'

'Tradition hasn't served us all that badly, Sally.'

'If you'll pardon my saying so, sir. Shouldn't it be what serves the public better, rather than what serves us best?'

'That's bolshie thinking, Inspector!' Doyle studied Speckle for a long time before he spoke again. 'Changing the world can be a lonely place, Sally. Are you sure you want to take it on? In Charlie Johnson you'll be losing a good copper.'

'I know that, sir.'

'Talk to him and Rochester again, eh. I'll misplace Johnson's transfer request for a couple of days. And Jerry Cranton's taken some leave to sort himself out. Lot of ground to make up with the missus.'

Speckle was pleased that her exhortations

that he should not quit had proved frutiful with Jerry Cranton.

'Oh, by the way, Andy Lukeson's on his way home, you'll be glad to hear.'

She was.

'Dozed off and fell off his chair. Got chucked out by Chief Superintendent Glass, the course organizer.'

Frank Doyle was still laughing when Sally Speckle was leaving and the phone rang. 'Doyle. Hello, Glass.' He frowned furiously. 'Because Lukeson didn't complete the course, the cost comes out of Loston's budget!'

DI Sally Speckle closed Doyle's door quietly. Walking along the coridoor, she began to laugh.

* * *

Ms Matterson opened her front door, surprised on seeing Sally Speckle on her doorstep again. 'I was just passing by, Ms Matterson,' she lied, reckoning that had she not Ms Matterson would not take kindly to thinking that her call was a charity call. She was a proud woman. 'Thought I'd check on you. Everything all right?'

Ms Matterson's eyes beamed warmly. 'So kind of you to take the time, Inspector. Would you like a cup of tea?'

'I'd love one, Ms Matterson.'

'Do come in, Inspector. And you must call me Emily.'

'And you must call me Sally.'

Ms Matterson sighed contentedly. 'Sally, it is. Like your tea strong or weak?'

'Strongish, Emily.'

Emily Matterson led the way along the hall, spritely. 'Strongish it shall be, Sally.'

THE END

Other titles published by
The House of Ulverscroft:

OLD BONES

J. A. O'Brien

When skeletal remains of a female are found in Thatcher's Lot, Loston CID is involved and DI Sally Speckle and her team investigate. The remains have been in the ground for five years — disturbingly, there were several women who went missing around that time. The missing women come from divergent backgrounds, but the skull has evidence of expensive dental care which Sally hopes will help to identify the remains. However, due to DC Helen Rochester's astuteness, the other women come into focus and unlikely suspects emerge. Now it starts to become a murder investigation within a murder investigation . . .

PICK UP

J. A. O'Brien

Jack Carver is experiencing the most horrible of all nightmares: being an innocent man who is the prime suspect in the brutal murder of two women. Forensic evidence is found at both crime scenes, which implicates Carver. And when the police request that he should come forward, he goes on the run instead. He is finally apprehended, but an incident from Carver's past shakes his absolute certainty that he is not the killer. Then he is charged with murder. Can DS Andy Lukeson prove his innocence when a chance incident prompts him to reassess the case?

A GAME OF MURDER

Ray Alan

Guests arrive at Stafford House for a Saturday evening buffet followed by party games, which include a game of murder. But they are unaware that a real murder has been planned, and that in turn is followed by a second death. Detective Inspector Bill Forward arrives to find there are eighteen suspects at the scene. Only after much patient investigation and strange leads can he bring the case to a surprising, unexpected conclusion.

MURDER IN BARE FEET

Roger Silverwood

Detective Inspector Angel must investigate a strange case where both the murderer and the murdered man are without shoes. The victim was a millionaire, adored by beautiful women, particularly the Frazer sisters, who put sparkle into his life and showed him how to spend his money. An antique dealer and his son are the prime suspects, but they have a rock solid alibi. At the same time, Angel has to investigate a flood and an armed robbery at the Great Northern Bank, involving millions of pounds. Inspector Michael Angel finds his investigative powers are tested in this most unusual case . . .

THE UNFORGIVING EYE

Beth Andrews

Returning from their honeymoon, John and Lydia Savidge are offered an extraordinary challenge: they are given three days to discover who killed Sir Benedict Stanbury, master of Fallowfield. Could the hapless stable hand accused of the crime really be guilty? Perhaps it was Sir Benedict's hoydenish niece or her mercenary mama? Or could it have been the suspicious solicitor or the frightened governess? Almost everyone had a motive for murder, but nobody can provide an alibi. Lydia and John have to unravel the tangled skein of perverse relationships and eccentric personalities before the startling truth is finally revealed.

THE UNKNOWN

James Pattinson

Mrs Craydon was taken with the idea of digging up the history of the family. And once started she became more enchanted by the project. Even her husband George, having once seen the ancient photograph of a most attractive girl, long since dead, developed an interest in the family genealogy. The only snag was that even Great-Aunt Maud, the owner of the photograph, had no idea what had happened to the beautiful girl named Isabella. Apparently she had completely vanished and to the rest of the family had simply become The Unknown. Would the mystery ever be solved?